BUGHOUSE BLUES

A Novel

Peter Thompson

Published in North America and Europe by Running wild press. Visit
Running Wild Press at www.Runningwildpress.com Educators, Librarians,
book clubs (as well as the eternally curious), go to
www.runningwildpress.com

Paperback ISBN 978-1-955062-14-5
Ebook ISBN 978-1-955062-15-2

May I, for my own self, song's truth reckon
--Ezra Pound, from
his version of *The Seafarer*

This narrative is dedicated to the few who relieve the pain of the many

Can we say that Dorothea Dix, the great reformer, had a hand in the design of this hospital? Built in her time, it certainly had the vast porches—meant to induce both physical and mental health—of the Dix-inspired St. Elizabeths, in Washington, DC.

Dix's theories are sometimes summed up as "moral," but the word's meaning was broader in the nineteenth century. While it implies kind and enlightened treatment, Dix was equally interested in physical environment and theories of holistic health. The hospital at hand has at times paid homage to her, and for some—mainly those who can spend all day out on the grounds—it is a lovely place. Her theories have succumbed to overcrowding and to waves of new ideas: diagnosis-specific housing, biological emphasis in pathology, psychotropic drugs.

While unspeakably grim in some areas, our hospital—like many humane structures of its era—has no perimeter walls to keep patients in. In fact some hospitals have added walls to keep the rest of us out—to keep us from raiding the fruit trees and gardens of the vast old greenswards.

This tale could just as well be called: Walls Beyond

Chapter 1

Rhodes killed the old Triumph under a straggly red maple and sat for a moment. He listened to the last genteel cough, a few creaks from the body, a faint ticking from under the hood. The bonnet.

He did this because these seconds, before he turned to face the Stack, were precious.

Standing by the car, his hand resting on the canvas top raised against a late April shower, he gazed up at the building that towered on its hillock, high above the rest of the asylum. A monstrous hulk of dark brick. Its embracing elms now gone except for one beauty by its side, a tree that lenited but failed either to embellish or to soften with nature's promise of entropy. How did this building, Harrison Rhodes, Psychiatric Health Worker 1, often wondered, manage to project both despair and institutional calm, containing, as it did, rack upon rack of hebephrenic gibberings, inconsolable moanings, soul-rent wailings.

As he put his foot on the first of the many steps, the old anxiety set upon him. The building seemed to give him one last chance, "Think very carefully, whippersnapper, before you enter here." Loss of feeling, loss of self, loss of world. A twelve-step program of abdication. And then the massive door, the last one that wouldn't require a key.

Chapter 2

Strange, approaching the ward he didn't think about the individuals, almost couldn't focus, as he did on the drive home in the winding starry night. The fantastic refinement of their alienation.

Colby the Shiteater, Moose, Iggy, Billy Beans, Beauchemin and his compulsion about glass, Long John, Davey Doucette (The Great Entertainer), Jungle Jim, Stan Mikita (hockey helmet, seizure disorder). And the eternal mystery of Anson Fowler's elegant mind.

Using his keys, and making sure their thick twine was in place, Rhodes first entered an abandoned ward, dim and smelling not of psychic horror, but simply of wax and Lysol. Letting himself through another door he strode quickly through another disused ward whose green linoleum was brightened by a few more lamps, but shadowed by the nurses' station. This served only admin purposes and was propped up by quite a bevy of granite-faced nurses. Odd, in these times (this was Rhodes in his late twenties, before his years as a teacher which the Gentle Reader may know from later chronicles), that you didn't use some mechanical or electronic gizmo to sign in for work at exactly 2:50 pm. You just got stared at with unveiled suspicion (especially if you were young, male, and fairly new at it all) and noted down.

It was in the stairwell that the sound-track picked up, the young Psychiatric Health Worker breathed deep and cast a longing glance through the few windows that weren't meshed over with thick wire.

The ornate, white trim on glowing brick buildings, and distant elms, the lonely elders, the small elm groups conversant, were eloquent about the wasted spring evenings, the summer of work to come. Huge, airy porches on most of them—the Stack had none—where unruly patients had been hosed down in the days before tranquilizing drugs. The calmer wards and their verandas beckoned.

At the third floor door of B Ward, Rhodes went full pro, wedged a foot against the door and, moving chin and nose out beyond the door's edge in case of treachery, twisted the heavy key.

Chapter 3

Well, what do you expect to find behind that door? Of a Thursday afternoon? One month on the job? The thrill of creative novelty, brilliant psychosis decorating the very air with its rococo? A new face or two on this "chronic" ward? A swell of Albert Schweitzer-Mother Teresa compassion lifting every moment of the eight hour shift? A summer love?

Hah, a harsh shoot-down there, though a new charge nurse was supposed to appear on Monday.

No, what's more likely to hit you is the familiar summer-job drill of having to work closely with yahoo colleagues you'll never see again, combined with mental patients' fawning and sudden, but artless, violence. And that smell: instant coffee, cigarette smoke, old urine.

But let's be even less concrete about it. A little exposition. What had weighed on Rhodes in recent days was the *what am I doing here* feeling that had fairly quickly replaced the *well, isn't this an adventure and a damn altruistic one too, me lad*. Everyone shared this disillusionment (all except the most brutal hillbilly staff): what do I actually *do* to help these people. But for Rhodes, it was also *so this is the appropriate endorsement of my choice of college major* (Classics), the one job avenue that wasn't barricaded with every type of stop sign, highway cone, sawhorse, and blinking red light? Because, on the most serious note, this was the job that paid, that kept him in Pabst, gas for the Triumph, and the odd

4

root vegetable. The other gig—mid-year replacement teaching Latin at a third-rate boarding school a bit to the north—was mainly remunerated, as a faculty member said, with "Dog food coupons and a bunch of laughing gas." So where the teaching gig might go was imponderable. And of further weight was the let-down, motoring down the highway after the half-day of teaching, the contrast between his evening clientele and the alert and winning students, the absolutely glowing companions of his morning. A tale for another day, perhaps, but harken to the shift—from goofy buoyant promise to medicated posture, "stereotyped gestures," worn-out slippers.

And so, there was much to this door in Rhodes's life. The extremely unsettling interview he'd had with the headmaster stayed with him all spring, impinging, as it did, on any decisions about the following year. Then, on the other hand, B Ward seemed more and more like a fate he needed to escape. He would, in fact, have to decide about more teaching before late spring—that is, if his interactions with beaming kids not ten years his juniors were not deemed too outrageous. Was the very large and wantonly intimidating headmaster likely to pay him more than his PHW salary once it was bumped above Trainee?

Much to consider. Much distraction, and distraction can be fatal when you're keying the B Ward door.

Quiet. But only relative to the high-pitched greed that would sound an hour later, when that area was used for smoking. They smoked on the ward, every two hours, timed to avoid change-of-shift. For decades an inalienable right of the mental patient, being (well, aside from masturbation and choking on steamy hotdogs and the other grim fare) the only pure moment: the golden minutes when time was judged at its true measure, when generosity abounded, when allostatic pleasure seemed to waft up from the floor, when a self-administered drug (perhaps that was the key) made the raver feel centered and lighter in his slippers. The filthy institutional secret: this was a way to shape

5

behavior, a way to punish, a way for staff to get the foulest chores done by someone else.

SMOKERS!

The bugle call every two hours, the mad shuffle (those who'd behaved themselves) toward the head of the ward.

And here, Rhodes saw as he looked quickly around the door before opening wide, there was only Iggy. In a corner, barely glancing at Rhodes, showing little of the curiosity the more with-it always showed at change-of-shift. And he was more with-it, oh yes. A sociopath, thin, oily, shifty of eye and shank, and with a personal hygiene that kept him well and truly in the pariah state that he craved. One Iggy, who long ago, according to the veterans, had been called The Iguana. Now, just Iggy. This time no manipulative harangue, only silent plotting.

"Finley," Rhodes greeted him. His trademark, calling patients by their actual names rather than the nicknames his colleagues crafted to lighten the psychic load.

As he approached the nurses' station, he realized most of his crew wasn't there. He decided to make the rounds, a necessary step before letting the day shift go. Before the Charge Aide would let them go, that is. As he slipped in and out of rooms, TV bay, bathrooms, he appeared—with lanky frame, thick dark mop and perhaps too scholarly steel-rims—less like a PHW and more like a very young shrink. This was also because he wore pressed pants—tough Dickeys, the knees able to stand hours of wrestling on the floor without tearing—and a decent shirt with a collar. This get-up, like the phrase "charge aide" ("aide," generally, had been upgraded to Psychiatric Health Worker), was a bit of a throw-back. Most, including the younger nurses, now wore jeans and battle-ready tee-shirts. Rhodes's mood and attire were still crisp as he checked for day shift sloth: a turd kicked under a bed, puddles, urine or otherwise, a pile of clothes that meant someone was "denuditive" which meant, of course, that it was the day shift's job to get the clothes back on.

He thought, too, about the question of the day's Charge. The mood of the whole evening depended on this; a bad Charge Aide made the hours drag for staff, but also, in cases of rare talent, made the whole ward jumpy—got the whole population of patients to accede to their worst obsessions, compulsions, delusions, anxieties, acrobatics, histrionics and sexual crimes. All the way till bedtime. When you staggered out to the parking lot sighing, "I can't do this anymore. This is like… a fucking mental hospital."

Back at the nurses' station, Rhodes saw that only his buddy, Jimmy Galt, was there. He asked Jimmy, "Hey, is Van Charge, or what?"

This was not the question of the day for Jimmy. The question of the day was, "We're not getting the new nurse, I heard, d'you hear? You hear we're getting Mavis again?" The burning injustice behind this quandary being that the new charge nurse, due Monday, one had thought, was said to be a virtual Helen of Troy. Which, in this venue, and even out into the surrounding counties, simply meant she didn't weigh two hundred pounds and could read a newspaper.

But let's dwell on Van for a second. This is stocky Gus Van Hoek, with reddish face, strawberry hair, and permanently startled expression. Rhodes had tried calling him Captain Hook, but the veterans had stared him down on that one. Some back-story about being drummed out of a family business, a tad more education than his peers at the hospital, a tale of failing at a franchise business locally, and now this. And a crew who took exception to the out-of-state feel of his moniker, along with the vaguely honorific aspect of the "Van." So, a touch mockingly, they just called him "Van."

Now, Rhodes was actually agnostic on the Van question. That is, the possibility that he was the devil incarnate, which should be taken to mean someone who would rat you out for hitting patients, was two-faced with the nurses, punished you with the foulest ward chores. Let's just say Rhodes was politically neutral on the man. Because he'd seen worse, in his short tenure, especially when pulling overtime on other wards. Van was maybe wound a little tight, but played it all straight. And he didn't, himself, hit patients. A plus in Rhodes's book. He'd given Rhodes a humorless and incredibly thorough orientation to the ward, and had always been fair.

Soon the whole team had arrived. It varied, because people rotated weekends off. But pretty much Rhodes's faves: Filbert (really Phil, but so named on account of size and high voice, a good soul); Donny Drouin, wiry Vietnam vet, tough, short legs, fast-walking, smart aleck; Dick Knight, tall, dark, easy-going, perhaps utterly without moral thoughts, the man most comfortable in his own skin that Rhodes had ever met.

Filbert, almost-on-the-spectrum, was intensely interested in Apples and Macs, owned an Eve. Drouin was going through a divorce that was, let's just say, colorful. Knight had starred on Bradford West's state-champion basketball team.

And Rhodes. He'd had a couple of months to fit in, had kept his nose clean, no visible reaction to the callousness of those around him, no wincing at the daily Poe-like knell of horror in the collective psyche of the ward. And he liked being on a team, did whatever he was told, tended to wear a not-too-cheesy smile. Because at that time Rhodes was a fairly affable type, wide-eyed at the world, damn glad to be in it instead of in school, ready to try anything, not yet seething at the innumerable different types of irredeemable people, not yet wound tighter and tighter by all the brow-furrowing, cranium-tightening, brain-stem twisting, teeth-grinding, scrotum-winching, gut-souring, palm-itching, and knee-buckling stupidities and irritations of life, its endless and failing-to-interlock conundra, its soul-hollowing disappointments, its gall.

That came later.

And so, with some relish, he listened to the Day Charge's and Van's briefings, glanced at "the book" himself, flipped through the charts of the more floridly psychotic, including—but there was some question here—Anson Fowler, and then "smoked them" at four o'clock. Not a chore anyone minded—a change of scene at least. You had to learn which brand was whose (of those brought in by relatives) and who got the coffin-nails the State saw fit to provide. You held the wooden tray in one hand, lit ciggies with the other. The main trick, since the kitchen door was open at this point, was keeping Billy (nicknamed Beans) from flitting wraith-like into the kitchen and "drinking" half a jar of instant coffee crystals. Beans had an addiction—psychological, perhaps that's the word, since he rarely scored—to caffeine. Rhodes was learning that this was an example of "compulsion" as defined in the charts, compulsion at an All-Star level. Beans was fast. And if he scored, you had to cope (though he had never been known to speak and was almost a non-presence on the ward, not much of a handful), and you were dealing with someone who wouldn't sleep for two straight days.

So Rhodes had a quiet moment, absorbing his share of what is blandly called secondhand smoke and watching the patients' eyes roll back in bliss. At such times, settling in after an hour on the ward, he was apt to take a larger view.

As another loveless summer minced its way toward him, and he gave a thought to the summer-job-girlfriend, the vision that had always quickened his step in the spring. And the Grecian ideal of the new charge nurse peeked at him from behind an Ionic column. But was this to be endlessly repeated? Not questioning our luck here; more the idea, new to Rhodes, that maybe this wasn't how you advanced in life, how you grew a bit. The thing was, this had some connection to the whole chain of beautiful summers, that is, to their evanescence—to the fading not only of their future likelihood, but of their aimless joy. And, probing more deeply, creasing the brow more deeply as he straight-armed Billy out of the kitchen door, Rhodes saw the connection to another life-avalanche, another freezing mass overhanging and threatening to break loose: was this *not* a summer job? Was this a career, the first of the Career Stairs that would keep him on this campus, turn him into one of the grubby tee-shirted cynics who toiled their lives there? Was it an escape, or merely an endless quandary, that the other campus beckoned, the weird little boarding school up north? And embedded in this quandary was the dubious old sleight-of-hand of "maturity," which had, in turn, for people of all stripes, embedded itself in the hazy construct called "purpose in life." As if life itself were not such an utter...such a...such complete...

The catalyst for hours of appalled self-reflection was that the enormous and quite likely insane headmaster seemed to approve of Rhodes, and was making noises about a full-time position.

Back in the nurses' station, Jimmy was still on theme: "Harsh news, Harry boy, Mavis being charge nurse all summer. If true."

"Jimmy, I don't have my ear to the granite on such matters. No one tells me anything. And, aside from the glamorous prospect of...er, the prospect of...anyway, Mavis is at least the devil we know." Mavis LaCroix, a stone legend. A tale for another time.

But just then a ruckus, not enough to really arouse these two pros, but an interruption nonetheless.

"Looks like the Friday shit is starting early," Jimmy sighed, heading for the Dutch-door. The Friday Shit, subtly different from the Saturday Shit, but distinguished from all the weekday evenings by its pitch and violence, was often marked by the presence of cops.

Sure enough, new talent hauled in from the mean streets, this time in curious leg shackles: bushy-haired, wide-eyed and grinning, The Wild Man of Borneo.

Chapter 4

Wild Man persisted through all of Rhodes's last days on the ward with no other name. This was, in part, because you never addressed him by name, not being able to get a word in edgewise. The epithet certainly added to his aura. But what also surrounded him, for Rhodes, was the guilt that came from dehumanizing him this way. Every time Rhodes thought of looking up his name, he just never got around to it. And such was the slippery slope toward normal staff behavior.

Colby the Shiteater, Jungle Jim, The Great Entertainer, Moose—all of them—ceased to be people here. That was humanity's great gift to them—that they could live here unmolested by society, but at the cost of their humanity. Of their individuality as people. Initially it was their madness that robbed them, and what they lost was personality. A life of choices, self-entertainment, willful differentiation from others. All their personalities were gone—withered, in some, or sequestered, or long-forgotten. Thus the automatisms, soothing and repetitive gestures, robotic predictability. The missing part seemed an improbable common denominator of all the paranoia, auditory hallucinations, compulsions, and organic brain syndromes of the ward. Ghost or shadow were terms almost too romantically colorful for these unpersons.

But of course, they were people. A bare hint of which could be gleaned from their charts, with hometowns, sketchy diagnosis, details of family dust-ups that finally expelled them from society. Or, if you're Rhodes, you glean this from a little quiet contemplation. But when he sank into these moments, he was stunned by his own sins. That, quite aside from what therapeutic drugs did to the patients, the hospital's omissions and commissions elegantly combined, over every eight-hour shift, as one persistent injury to them. By failing to do anything to resuscitate these personalities the staff pushed them further and further from everything human.

What nagged at Rhodes was that he was part of it. Fifty patients every day, all minimalists (except when one or two "went high"), a certain sameness to how you dealt with them. As when taking the Wild Man of Borneo out of his locked room, naked (since, for months, he wouldn't tolerate clothes) for a bathroom break. His hair more and more like an Afro, his wide eyes probing *as if* he were interested in you, a generous smile, and no time for Rhodes's "And how are *you* doing today?" before this white, normally-shaped, twenty-year-old (history of drug use) started in.

"The buildings have such teeth. The pages of my window are stuck. When is the lovely soap? She has a baseball diamond in her hair. I'm so excited, I'm so excited. The chowder is *exquisite exquisite exquisite*! A psychoanalyst in his rectum? This will have to be rectified! Punctually! Funda*mentally*! *Analy*tically! How pro*found* linoleum is!"

So that Rhodes was soon weary and only relieved to turn a key on what was left of this person, to turn to the management of people who were even less.

Intimations, as you can guess, that this was a career whose every shift made *him* less.

Chapter 5

In college, an old advisor, Rancoeur, a scholar of French literature, had finally—and very kindly—wheezed, "Well, maybe what you thought you liked about doctoring was the service part of it." He said this while using what the French call "the ear finger" for its evolutionary purpose. "But there are other kinds of service."

Rhodes had always thought he would be a doctor. He'd pictured it so many times. Not exactly the intense diagnostic and intellectual part, or even the requisite and reassuring pose at bedside. More the other person's aching need part of it. Being able to do something about that. This had lasted through almost two years of higher ed.

But, as his advisor explained, teaching, or a number of other fields, could fill the bill. This was just as Rhodes was becoming entranced by language and some strange literature, and seduced by—of all things— the ancient Romans. He loved manipulating their crazy language, sure, but he really loved thinking about their plumbing. And military adventures. And architecture blazing in the Mediterranean sun. More and more he was beguiled by their rhetoric—because it was acting on people, it was making a world. He loved to picture Cicero or old Cato thundering along in the Senate, and he loved that the Romans revered their poets. More and more he loved the idea that he could make that world—he could make it real for students.

So now, after a few years of floundering around, he's staring that career in the face, and also falling back on a healing path, the medical world. And, in a way which—let's face it, as we come to know this guy—is typically indecisive, he feels as though there is a partition between the two paths. It's a very thin wall, having a thinness that offers the exciting prospect of plunging through it at any time. But it's translucent, not transparent. It's trans-something, suggestive of mutation. Also frustrating, because Rhodes could see everything on one side very clearly. He could next, at some point, up at the prep school for example, see everything on the other side. He could never hold the contents of both vistas at once. To, you know…make a decision.

Chapter 6

Well sir, just when you think life is never going to withdraw its rough peasant's boot from the first bend in your colon, you win the dang lottery. Sherrill Langdon, dark-eyed, helmet of black hair, petite (five-fiveish), nice color to her (these last two traits a bit rare in the land of Scots-Anglo-French settlers), and disquietingly stern. Her thin but natural eyebrows knit very slightly as she concentrated on her work. Calm, very professional, as the small roomful of aides concentrated on her fine little frame.

She didn't look anyone in the eye for a couple of days, but her upturned nose and the business-like slant of her small mouth were appreciated notwithstanding.

"Hey now," Galt murmured to Rhodes, "just when you think life—"

"Yeah, take it easy, Jimmy. This has got to be some kind of goddamn mirage. This can't be happening."

"Not to us, right? Not on B Ward! But I asked her—she's it, she's in the charge nurse rotation, this is her assigned ward."

"But look how fucking young she is! Do you think she finds twenty-seven-year-olds ancient?"

"Hah! Like unspontaneous, wheezy…"

"Hidebound, jaded…"

"Inflexible, uninformed…"

"Jimmy, we gotta keep our heads about us. This is a bit of a curve ball. I don't see how I'm supposed to concentrate."

"Like, on what, Harry, when's the last time you had to concentrate on anything around here?"

"OK, good point. But still. I can't take it. I'm staying out here on the ward. You go in there, get her talking or something. I need to adjust."

It should be understood that, fetching though she was, she was The Boss. And not just of this ward; she ran A and B Wards for the 3:00-11:00 shift, or even two shifts in a row. Ranking below the administrative nurse for the whole building, a nurse on day shift, the admirable Minnie Jewel. And Jewel, in turn, was below Doctor Burns who, in theory, diagnosed and designed therapy for the patients. But this ray of hope, this golden dew drop, this feverish new dawn, Sherrill, was the boss-person Rhodes had to not embarrass himself in front of. Because…well, for a couple of reasons.

The routine was you got on your feet, looked alert, checked the physical condition of the ward real quick twice per shift, when she "passed meds." That was, in fact, her main function, along with some paperwork, some probing of the charge aide and perusal of his book (doomed attempts to really know the souls and skills of the aides), and approving emergency moves like full restraints, "bolted chair," locked room. So when she came through, you looked sharp, and you stood by her separate Dutch-door as she gave out the medications (protected her, to be frank, but also made sure the meds were swallowed). You didn't get caught giving patients piggy-backs, eating the snacks their families had delivered, or, worst of all, reading. You were not to be seen reading the newspaper, or your Jean-Paul Sartre, a titty-mag (which the aides couldn't even dignify with its proper name, titty-mag, but instead called "fuck-books"). Your Updike.

At other times, when you were sure she had left, you kicked back. Rhodes watched her key the door near him, the one that led to the stairwell and down to A Ward, the women's crisis unit. He dragged one of the massive oak ward chairs to a spot where he could tip it back and see down both legs of his soup-green L-shaped precinct. Much food, puzzling hors d'oeuvres really, for thought.

He'd picked up that she was local, had obviously done alright, just about yesterday, in high school, was motivated. So she didn't just float in, Botticelli-style, on a seashell, though it felt like that. She had some kind of hellish family that spelled Cheryl this way, possibly after a TV actress.

When Rhodes saw Anson Fowler motionless at the far end of the ward, his hand resting on the thick screen, he realized how much this Sherrill had distracted him from the most interesting project he'd had in a while. And then he thought, "Well let's just simmer down here, take things at a natural pace." The best way to see what she was made of—was she more than a gaudy flash in the brain pan?—would be to see her interacting with patients. All in good time. She'd build up (knowing the patient's measured ways) to a chat with Anson Fowler.

At times like this you couldn't say—with the weird stasis, the lull in Rhodes's always problematic momentum, the sudden alertness to perduring life everywhere—that there was a new silence. No. What there was was a strange hum, the susurrus of The Stack. Composed less of the building's machinery and the groaning of various fixtures in the heat than of the psychic aberration of hundreds of mental patients. A low sound, barely discernible—when B Ward inexplicably quieted down. The sound you get, it seems, when you mix moaning, sighing, self-slapping, shuffling, flesh-digging, complaining, plotting, snoring, and peeing against walls. And *not* the sound of spiritual transcendence, *not* the sound of Rhodes communing with his inner light.

Rhodes was drifting off into this sound when Anson Fowler moved away from the distant window and back into his thoughts. He wondered if the patient would stride toward him—tall, hawk-eyed, patrician—for one of his talks.

"Depressive," "assaultive," were all the background to be found in his chart, and these were observations from twenty or thirty years back, when something went haywire in the life of this educated man and he hit the wards. Now about fifty, he seemed to Rhodes like the adult in the place. The much older patients were too wacky, so was the staff half the time. Anson Fowler exerted a strange pull on Rhodes, seeming to know something nobody else did—seeming somehow in control. This, along with a spellbinding delivery, as his diatribes against the doctors rattled off the walls, as he impugned their intellects, their integrity, their humanity. It constantly made Rhodes question Fowler's presence; why wasn't he fulminating in a court of law or something?

What was his real story?

It should be noted, if the alert reader has not already understood this, that the two crisis wards were single sex. The staff was all-male in the case of B Ward, except when the charge nurse was around. And there were patients who assaulted on other wards because they wanted to come to this more Spartan (and some would say infamous) unit—and they wanted this because they didn't want any women around. There was a theory that Anson was of this group. A chronic group.

"Harry, when last we spoke I was describing to you the imponderable iniquity of the diagnostic staff here, in particular that ham-fisted veterinarian Dr. Ubu." (This is Dr. Igbo, a well-meaning Nigerian of long ago who had admitted Anson.)

"I well remember, Anson. But you have Dr. Burns now."

"I will come to him *in turn*," Anson spat out, giving Rhodes the sharp look that had often meant he was not worthy of the rest of the paragraph. His discourses were well-ordered and brooked no interruption. His cadence, when not rising to a Ciceronian pitch, was that of a long-time prisoner who has carefully memorized the whole thing.

"It was Dr. Ubu, as I'm sure I've told you, that initiated a hellish concatenation of crimes against me, against my mental condition. He put me in Cilley Building, for one thing, with those…with *those*…And then a further barrage of injuries and all manner of peregrination authored by the same pygmy brought me to the sewer (pronounced slowly and distinctly, "syoo-wer") of Rumford Building (The Stack) and that mountebank Herr Blisters (Burns)."

"OK, I'm following you so far. But what is the latest outrage?"

"You would think that in the modern age—though we speak of an era their minds might not be acquainted with—they would let a person have written correspondence with his family."

"Oh, right. I think you mentioned a sister…"

"She doesn't write me. But they won't let *me* write *her*." Here, he looked away from Rhodes with a somewhat unusual expression. Just the one you would expect, actually, but that wistful look was so unlike the daily run of his expressions, or non-expressions—rhetorical fixtures, really—that it made Rhodes thoughtful.

The typical staff response to Fowler was a slight intimidation by his vocabulary and bearing, a feeling which squirmed unhealthily beneath the veneer of contemptuous apathy directed at virtually all patients. Our man Rhodes, of course, had long been leery of falling into this kind of casual disregard, and was particularly indignant that it could be applied to someone as interesting as Fowler. The interest, it will be observed, grew not only from his murky background and education level, but also from the conundrum of his illness. Was he in fact the sanest one there? Was he in complete control in some way? In a way that wouldn't arise once among a million "normal" people?

There was the relevant case of a patient a friend had described, at another hospital. You could spy on him all the day long—you wouldn't find a hint of insanity. It was odd that he wore some kind of knee-socks and hiked his pants into them, giving the effect of knickerbockers. The pocket protectors and vast array of pens, and the constant companionship of a transistor radio, those were well within the sane spectrum. Wearing a sports jacket was a bit odd, in a public loony bin. But the point was his calm, punctilious bearing. His placid reading of a newspaper he had delivered. A new staff member might rattle him momentarily by showing the endemic contempt for patients. To be sure, he went through some kind of inner wrenching as he turned his gaze from the horrors that erupted on the ward. But he had assumed dignity, and it was carefully demonstrated and preserved—even by most staff. So Rhodes's friend never got to the forbidding bottom of this: his presence—as opposed to his release. It was clear that he had made the hospital his world. He had remade his world. It was how he maintained control. It was a world—and who are we to say it wasn't also a sanity—he was able to sustain. And this because...his insanity flared only beyond the gates? Because, in a way which could justly be called sane, he saw more fully than most of us the horror of the world?

"I haven't seen anything about that in your ch—in your records. I mean I..."

"Herr Blisters manages to make the letters disappear. You know how mail is handled here. He can do what he wants." The normal stance for Fowler was to look far across the smoking area or out a window when talking to someone. Occasionally he looked toward the other, but then only at a spot exactly in the center of that person's forehead. So it was an odd end to the conversation, a complete fade-out of the rhetoric, when he seemed for a split second to look in Rhodes's eyes, as the young champion said,

"Why don't I bring it up with Burns?"

Chapter 7

We now find the increasingly anxious mental health worker, Rhodes, in the tunnels under the campus. Mid-evening, having volunteered to do "Night Doors," locking the various connections and bulkheads in the tunnels. A spooky setting, even at mid-day.

The tunnels were no doubt carved at the 1850s creation of the institution as a way to transport patients from building to building in the winter. Later they ran steam pipes from the central plant to heat most of the buildings. Later still, they were strapped with electrical cable. The whitewash did little to brighten them. The floor seemed to be of beaten earth. In the oldest section, under the Main Building, there were rooms, more like cells, that always gave Rhodes a shudder. An iron ring fixed to the floor of one of them was especially troubling.

You quickly lost your bearings. You had to proceed by routine, counting your left and right turns, to do your job properly (chasing patients back to the wards and locking up) while not disappearing forever. He had paused this time at a particular corner, listening for the vigorous slurping, and had known by the absence of that telltale that Joanne wasn't richer by a pack of Marlboros this evening. He stifled the "Enough of that, Joanne, back to the ward, both of you!" that was almost automatic.

Only one sharply sloping floor gave a clue—it clearly led to Phelps Building. After Rhodes had locked one side of the bulkhead, he paused, knowing that behind him was the maw of a little used tunnel, completely dark, that supposedly led to the Medical Building but was rumored to have offshoots. What drew Rhodes a few steps into this horror-movie stretch of architecture was as unclear to him as everything else. Turning what he judged to be 180 degrees he could still see the reassuring light of the branch he had come from. So he stood still, somehow enjoying the soundless murk, slightly apprehensive to be sure, but starting to appreciate the chance to think something through.

There was his annoyance, of course, that he'd had "bolted chair" duty right when Sherrill was passing meds. The bolted chair, the old oak model bolted to the floor out on the ward, had leather restraints for these special assignments. The theory was that a particular patient needed to be watched and also restrained, and no one could be spared to watch him in his room. In some cases it was more that he needed restraint, but was "acting out" (more on this pop diagnosis later) because he wanted his room—and the chair was to force him to socialize. The PHW had to sit close by in case of a nimble and vicious attack by another patient.

So Rhodes had had to watch the strapping, wide-faced, hippy-haired Jimmy Galt leering (oops, *assisting*) at the Dutch-door of the medication cabinet.

But he quickly shook this off—spot of childish envy for heaven's sake. Grow the hell up. What swelled like a malevolent mushroom in the dark of the side tunnel was the interview with Burns.

Rhodes had met Burns when first hired. Pretty much in passing, not in his Main Building office. He'd learned that you rarely dealt with him, that he wasn't all that forthcoming about actual diagnoses, and, finally, that he was (had practiced as) a pediatrician, not even a psychiatrist. A second meeting was the mandatory one-month review, to see how the new hire's work was coming along. This had been in the office.

Let's see what one expects, right? From an office like this. A serious bank of files. A bookcase, clearly medical in content. A bright, modern, positivist air about the place, a clean floor, the feeling that Science presided and that the administrator had one of those clear, open faces owned by people who have swept away all the neurotic cobwebs. Maybe a desk statue of the goddess of wisdom (Minerva, to Rhodes).

But no. The effect was so opposite that Rhodes had stepped back a pace, to make sure he was in the right room. Nor could he prove this by simply looking at Dr. Burns, so gloomy was the lighting. He peered, half stumbled forward, until a fat hand motioned him to a chair.

He made out a not-especially-Rorschachian pattern on an oriental rug, so shabby that it screamed at him either *heirloom* or *cheap consignment shop*. A tank, and one fish of a dubious shade of brown, took up most of the wall behind Burns. This fish, as it moved spectrally through its fronds and grottos, enjoyed more light than did the room at large. The other walls thronged with books which a glance revealed to be too delicate to be medical or even pop-science. Not even a DSM, the fabled *Diagnostic and Statistical Manual of Mental Disorders*. The run of them that started by Rhodes's left arm began with the *Oxford Book of English Verse* and then flowered into a long stretch of examples of this, none of them the good stuff, the Jonson, Herrick, the Metaphysicals, just the pining, wilting stuff. The place looked like the country squire's library of a lost era.

Oh there was a statue alright. On the desk, an African male with engorged genitals. One patient after another was forced to hide his reaction to this while peering around the penumbra of the doctor's blotter trying to avoid his fat-lidded eyes.

A key observation, during that first visit, as Rhodes made the necessary adjustment to the light, was how much of the sun was blocked by the doctor's outlandish body. Big shoulders and a bull neck, a double cannon ball of a head. But still you couldn't say this was a man who "carried it well." This was a great fat person, with many bits pressing and distorting both clothes and furniture, along with other bits trying to lift off like saddlebags flapping on a horse. The whole affair gave an impression of tremendous weight, and not the "jolly innkeeper" kind, not the "surprisingly agile" kind. No, the steamingly adamant, unmovable kind.

This was also the visit when Rhodes noticed the speech. A pendulous drag to it, slow, minatory at times. But the kicker was the initial "r"s. As in Rhodes.

"So, Mr....." What followed, as with the surprising number of other words that start with "r," was a fleeting panic in the eyes, then a low, soft grunt, like a very scaled-down version of an indigenous person of lore preparing to hurl himself off a cliff, "...*guh*," then an "oo-" that led into the "w" that would have to do. "Mr. *guh*... oo-w-Whodes, an uneventful month, I take it? So far?" Some of the probing that followed this suggested Burns wanted information, didn't actually know how the ward had been managing. "I hear you're adjusting well."

"Oh sure. Great team. Getting to know the patients, you know, it's going OK. A bit hard to learn anything, anything substantial, about some of the pa—"

"Because, heh, *guh*...oo-Whodes, things can get a little, shall we say, *festive*, on B Ward."

"Oh! Yeah," (weak chuckle), "so I've heard."

"B Warned!" (This pun was standard, relating to the ward.) "Ha! But..." the man creaked, like a dangerous party balloon, forward, "of course, you'll be getting Mavis, Mavis LaCroix, as charge nurse. Solid move. This is what's needed, speaking of your 'great team,'" (he put a gratuitous and poisonous irony into this) "she is what's called for. Somewhat *guh*...oo-westrictive, perhaps, but just what the doctor (heh) ordered."

Some of the threat of this interview had dissolved, a few weeks later, when Sherrill Langdon got the nod over LaCroix, and Rhodes, frozen like an old catatonic here in the deepest tunnel, now mused about his luck, but also about how she'd just been driven from his mind by Burns. By thoughts of an office visit.

It wasn't just that Rhodes had promised something to Anson Fowler. It was that Burns, shuffling along a Main Building hallway, had recently wheezed, "You'll need to make an appointment with me. Next week. Need to have a chat."

Brooding a bit darkly, he climbed back up to the ward, only ten minutes late. This would have been unobserved, except that his strapping brand of wrestling prowess was needed for the donnybrook in progress.

Chapter 8

The problem was Colby the Shit Eater. Now, in your static situation, your moments of professionally obtained peace and order, when someone was manning the bolted chair, no one was restrained naked on a rubber mattress, the nurse wasn't around, smokes were done and Iggy wasn't hatching a new plot, you'd have made sure that if Colby was out and about he was corralled down at the far end of the ward, not headed for the smoking area, not tempted by a hefty floater in one of the doorless stalls.

But something had gone wrong. He must have been allowed a bathroom break right before bed and a PHW—likely Donny Drouin, whose commitment to the job varied jaggedly—hadn't kept an eye on him. So now, you see, the problem is getting a fat turd out of his hand while he's squeezing it and you're wrestling and chastising (belatedly threatening, trying behavior modification on this, the most compulsive of all patients). You can see the difficulty. This business, the rare times it happened, ended badly, very badly, for all concerned.

While Jimmy and Rhodes felt that their hands would never again be clean, at least the crew had amassed clean towels from the laundry room—mostly against the heat that continued to build, all the way to eleven o'clock, in the upper floors. Everyone stood panting, too sweaty even to sit down, and staring at Live-Free Lenny. Among the yellow vinyl chairs, old wood cabinets, and racks of blue plastic "charts," he was reaching into his pants and daubing his thighs with baby oil, and had not lent his er…weight to the fracas. The only fan had been turned toward him. Van, a man who particularly minded sweating, was always tense at Lenny's regal presence.

Live-Free was Christened not so much as a nod to rugged individualism as to his native cleverness in cadging free goods, mainly from the hospital. Any skin cream needs waited until he was on shift, likewise foot-powder needs, the stashing of spare cigarettes, a yen for a state-supplied hot dog or burrito. A pyramidal mass of a man, nonetheless with small hands and a fastidious way of examining and enjoying the fruits of his petty-thievery.

Lenny leaned back in anticipation of doing nothing for eight hours, an overtime replacement for Filbert who had rotated off. Trunk-like limbs, a giant beach ball belly tapering toward a bald pin-head. The whole package was on the swarthy side, which forced Rhodes to picture Lenny in a beach chair, among the discarded washing machines and transmissions in the yard of his horrible little house (Rhodes had been by), Lenny, taking the sun.

This psychiatric worker's only known talent was an incredible range (in the melodic sense) of farts. Always startling, always somewhat theatrical, and—especially the high, thin timbre—improbable. Rhodes had tried to rename him Fart-Free Lenny, but the veterans had given that thumbs down. When he tried to make a comeback, in the nickname department, with Lenny Two-Tones they gave that one the stone eyes too. The man's range could rattle the whole nurses' station with a basso profundo, like an English cathedral organ, move up through circus clown horns and all the Peter and the Wolf stunts, and on to a kind of Minuteman's trilling fife.

There was nothing to do now, as Rhodes realized with sinking spirits, but fill out the patients' charts. He noticed the pile, all done and slightly less than his share, next to Lenny's chair. The betting was that

27

every one of them said "Quiet and cooperative," and nothing more.

This was the old pro's game: well, why wouldn't they all be quiet and cooperative, having enough Stelazine, Thorazine, Mellaril or Haldol in them to take a Napoleonic stallion off the battlefield, set an elephant on his keister? Along with this dose, being what is called "institutionalized." That is, having achieved their ward of choice, unless on furlough from a home ward for hitting someone with a cribbage board. Or having given up all desire, except for the food and cigarettes which were forthcoming, or having forgotten the "outside," having forgotten emotions, having forgotten that they once wanted to leave.

Lenny wasn't the only one guilty of this belittling sloth. As Rhodes let his head flop back on the chair, with most of the charts on his lap, done, he asked himself what in the world he would say about Fowler's last eight hours. And, as the magic moment of 10:50 approached, he let it all go. All the things he felt he needed to think hard about: an opening gambit with Sherrill (brief, professional), his teaching gig, the humanity that clearly still throbbed in Fowler, whatever was on Burns's mind.

He thought only of his well-earned thing—charging in the old Triumph, top down in the cool air, a dash between tall poplars and their frame of the faithful summer stars.

In Fowler's chart he scribbled, "Quiet and cooperative."

Chapter 9

The mid-year interview with the headmaster had been, of course, a nightmarish affair. Combining as it did the shock of the actual encounter with the quandary and self-loathing over having accepted the two-class load and jocular salary offer.

Barnes, headmaster of the small red brick school nestled in the hills, was a towering—if they have fat towers? do they?—figure, with a wide face of lava-flow lard, and giving off an awful scent blended of cold cuts and talcum powder. He had stared at Rhodes's c.v. so long it seemed he thought he was alone. Then, pitching forward in a way that made his oddly Spartan desk groan, he had attacked Rhodes's judgment. "Classics? LATIN? This is what you majored in?"

Stunned, Rhodes fished for some sign of mirth in the horrid little pools of the headmaster's eyes. "Well, er...I mean...you *were* looking for a Latin teacher."

"I *know* what I was looking for. Am looking for—*still* looking," he added with a meaningful glance. "*My* question is," and here, since his girth was already straining at the desk, and the desk was actually a weighty affair, he telescoped his neck, opting to make himself denser, more bomb-like, and more threatening in that way, "how are you going to get along with the hockey coach?"

"The what?" Is this man artfully using *non sequiturs* as some kind of intelligence test, or free association assessment? Was he mad? Was he stupid *and* fat?

What followed was Rhodes batting back such questions exactly (thinking too hard) as he imagined a sane person would. With such gems, which all died a horrible death on Barnes's desk, as "Well gee, I don't know. I like hockey. Like it a lot. Bruins fan since Neely and Oates. I like to skate. In fact I skate like the...like the..."

"And how does $2,300 a course sound? Decent kids, two courses. You can have lunch here."

These words were the *open sesame* to the sane world, sounds that finally opened the office door, that meant a suddenly tired-looking Barnes was going to stop tormenting him and let him leave the building. Words that had played in a slightly unsatisfactory way in Rhodes's mind as he drove back to his apartment near the hospital.

And now, as he headed for his interview with Dr. Burns, Rhodes rounded a gothic series of corners in the Main Building and almost tripped over the man.

He was giving the patient Joanne what we hope was a fatherly pat on the head, murmuring, "Oh, how sharper than a serpent's thanks it is to have a toothless child. Alright, off you go now." He greeted our young hero's stutter-step with, "Ah, Mr. *guh*... oo-Whodes. *Guh*... oo-wight this way. A few things to chew over together."

"Yeah," Rhodes adopting buoyant tone, taking the initiative, "I have a few questions about some patients, for example An—"

Burns interrupted, "What's this about you working up north? Hm?"

"What...?"

"For the self-inflated blimp of a headmaster, my brother, Barnes. At Daniel Webster Academy. Half-brother. What's the story?" This was drilled out, as if pent up.

"Your..." They shared a what, a mother? Rhodes tried not to picture her.

"Half-brother. Though full jackass." He squeaked back, attempted to fold his hands behind his head, gave that up. "The man is a dangerous incompetent, on top of impulse control issues. In the clinical sense. Do you have a contract? This is not to be trusted. Do you? What's your plan?"

"Oh, well, I…Actually I got that job first, just two classes up there. But then I got this job, the real thing. I mean, not that the students are crazy and *these* people are too, I just mean. Well I mean, a full-time job. But I have a contract up there, for this year, so…"

"Toilet paper."

"Excuse me?"

"Just trying to help you here. The man is literally capable of having a bonfire with those contracts. Completely unpredictable. He's capable of lighting fire to the whole school in a fit of mania and dancing nimbly—well, not so nimbly—but gleefully over the embers. Listen," a change of register here, just as Rhodes was thinking the real raver was in front of him and he could ghost through the rest of the interview, "it's more involved than that."

Long pause.

"I could use more good staff here, I could use a little *education*, I don't know, a little more polish around here. The ward, as you may know, has an unsavory *guh*…oo-weputation—has even made the papers a few times. And now that this Beryl, or Meryl, Langston, or whatever, is one of the charge nurses, the thing could go to hell."

"Sherrill…"

"Whatever. A child. A waif. Is she going to mold this unit the way I want—I don't think so, pal. Hah! Has she ever seen one of our Saturday shindigs? You see her answering the Bell, like Mavis? On the actual deal, the B Ward Blow-out?" He seemed deeply depressed. Brightening slightly, "Anyway you are part of what I'm trying to *guh*… oo-weinvigorate here, you could be one of the building blocks. I need you to make up your mind, probation's over soon, get into Career Stairs. Look, up there it's yearly, capricious contracts from an arrant lunatic. Here your future is assured."

And that was the thing. Well, there was, lately, *the thing about* his future. What the hell did he want to do? Why did he feel he was losing something by deciding? Even Burns calling him, as no one else did, *Mr. Rh—*, or *Wh—* or whatever; is this what being twenty-seven was, you got called Mr., and were expected to have it all worked out?

But that wasn't THE thing that lingered.

"Your future is assured."

A certain finality, to be sure, linked to the problem just mentioned. But it was creepier. A certain affinity to the patients too, as Rhodes realized over the next few days, yes, that was it, even to the staff. In the mental hospital, in The Stack, everyone's *future…was assured.*

Chapter 10

Good Lord. So, given all this, some kind of break, or break-out, was called for. Get some perspective on the institution, on a lot of things, recreate a bit. And this could be done *along with* getting to know Nurse Langdon, if such a thing as a *date* could be arranged.

It was the unbelievable smoothness of the skin on her arms, and something childish, maybe the beginnings of a pout and then the chewing on the inside of her lip as she worked out some snafu in the Meds Book. These, it must be, were allotropes, and yes, childish ones, of what Rhodes called his "youth," and its receding. And he felt an awful sympathy for her, and not just fear and joy for her, as the poet says, but for him. Action!

So, feigning careless indifference, kind of ambling down the ward, but with an eye on the Meds door, he suddenly boxed out Jimmy Galt and helped Sherrill open it and then swing the lower half shut. The bar over which she served the pills and little cups, the elephant-gun doses. Jimmy wobbled off, yelling "Meds! Medic-*A*-tions!"

Rhodes offered, "Glad you're on tonight. We don't see enough of you!" Then, as she unlocked her cabinet without looking at him, he pulled back slightly with, "Love to know what you think of the place. If you have some insights." Now she almost looked his way, didn't speak. "Especially about some of the patients, You might know more than I do."

Colby had arrived at the Dutch-door. With a quick glance at his fingers, Rhodes greeted him cheerfully, peered into eyes beneath an incredibly low brow, called him by his first name (Seward). With the next series of patients, Rhodes put a brotherly hand on the shoulder of each, looked them full in the face, asked in his most pleasant voice, "You get that down alright? Hm? Did we swallow? Let me see that tongue, Davey," and so on.

He noticed that Sherrill was looking deeply into the eyes of each man. In the case of the towering Moose this took some doing. She wore a concerned and unhurried—and in this place and time you'd have to say that amounted to a *kind*—expression for each.

As she finished up and locked the white enameled door of the cabinet, she looked at Rhodes for the first time. This caused him to splutter, "You don't have office hours do you, like before the shift? I'd—"

"Oh," she cut him off, pausing meaningfully so that he would move away from the door, "I'm sure we'll run into each other. Honestly, I'm pretty clueless around here. All my experience was in Cilley Building," (a notorious warehouse). Then her first smile, but with a goodbye that, Rhodes felt, was as dismissive as it was trite.

"You know, one day at a time!"

Chapter 11

Anson Fowler threw back his leonine grey hair, tilted his fine features toward the sun, and, making sure of his audience with a sidelong glance, launched a typical fusillade:

"And so it was—and if you don't understand this, new boy, you should look into the history of this place—that the unhappy legions you know as *patients* (and how our patience is wearing *thin*) were drawn in a long, trudging file toward this sink-hole of the soul. Once here, of course, we were immobilized by the great ontological suction-pump that has robbed us of *being*. You have had a chance to observe the scene." There was no break here, no eye contact, as usual—no invitation to conversation. "The fact that our being has been sucked out of us is palpable on the ward, in the very smells and sounds that are left when the great machine of The Stack, relentlessly operated by Herr Blisters and his minions, has done its work. Look around you. To say nothing of the cold, intergalactic void of my own future—more on this, later—you can see what remains here of *life*, of life on the verdant earth, of the life of young bodies.

"Look at Long John, now a crumpled, stringless puppet. Look at The Great Entertainer, as you joshingly call him—yes, I've heard you— the man is a wind-up automaton. Look at Moose. God knows the soul of that man was vacuumed out long, long ago.

"One wonders if the souls of all these people—and mine too, I sometimes think—are *kept* somewhere, perhaps in glass cylinders in the tunnels, stored for some filthy use, or, in the opposite eventuality, for some massive intervention that will restore human wholeness." His fingers, as was often to be seen, now crept up the massive wires of the inside screen, hooked into them. "I tell you I can't *wait* for that day. It's not a day I have any sense of in *time,* or any optimism about in the realm of normal time, you understand. But a hard certainty, a constant awareness of its hard, certain existence in some dimension. A very present dimension. A dimension of clarity and a glinting, moral hardness—that I feel increasingly close to."

This kind of thing often left Rhodes in the dust, much as he wanted to follow. He had been fascinated at first, the way new hires were fascinated, by everything on campus. Then by the man's strange sanity. Then, especially, one day when Rhodes had said something careless and dismissive to Davey Doucette, The Great Entertainer, and Fowler had said, in the bored tone of someone reprimanding a child, "Don't talk to him that way. You didn't just meet him yesterday."

The oration had, for the moment, dried up. In fact these soliloquies all had the predictable rhythm and duration of set-pieces, though in other ways emotional and *ex tempore.* It's more that the man's psyche had a certain rhythm or duration of effort when it came to exposition. And Rhodes knew this to be the moment he should fess up: that he'd forgotten to press Dr. Burns about Fowler, his treatment, his letters to family and so on.

He burned with embarrassment. "I uh…" Fowler's head moved very slightly toward him, the tiniest recognition that he was being addressed, but more overt than usual. It could be that he was never going to ask, but had been waiting for this. "I forgot just now to talk to Burns about you. I mean I went in there intending to…He got very persistent, a bit loud, about other stuff, and…"

"And you were brain-burgled." Said with the bored, didactic tone Rhodes had heard before.

Fowler walked the length of the ward to another window.

Chapter 12

Spurred by something Fowler had said, Rhodes did look into the hospital's history. He'd had a shadowy glimpse of it in the tunnels, of course, and he also came to understand that, after the "decentralization" movement in the '60s, the population was down. He struggled to imagine how any of the patients he knew could be shipped out to "community mental health," pictured their exploding in that setting, saw that some would yearn to be back on the old campus. He also lent his awed imagination to a former campus not only more crowded, but minus the benefit of modern medication.

The old vets, thinking back to those days, guys like Live-Free Lenny, would gaze wistfully through the unmeshed windows of the nursing station upon the tail of their lives fleet in the evening sky, and get moist-eyed describing the special shrill tone of the wards back then before the advent of psychotropic drugs.

"You seen it all, Lenny…"

"You better know it," he'd say. Pronounced, *You bettah know ut.* And Lenny would veer from the misty to the sternly didactic, saying this to Rhodes, as the newest team member, with a piercing look.

But why? *Why* had he better know it, why did he need to know about fighting, back then, foot and fist, with the unmedicated paranoiacs?

Why?

Still, it seemed important, he wasn't sure why, to think of the hospital's uniqueness in time and place. It stored the psychotics that, in his limited travels (Africa and France, visiting Roman ruins) he'd found to have the same gestures and facial tics all over the world. This seemed to him a very odd conjunction of time, space and the genome. He also realized with a shock that his patients *were* the history of the stolid bricks and neglected greensward; some of them had been there a half century.

This kind of rumination, triggered by several axes of theme and antics on the ward, got him thinking about his place in time, his future.

PHW 2, was that it? Or teacher. He pictured a grayer, rounder version of himself in the latter role, trying to fart inaudibly in a small office and hopelessly eyeing a stack of student papers while his tired mind struggled for a reason to put them off. Then he pictured himself waddling onto the wards, stooped, careless with keys (a fireable offense), greeting no one but the charge aide.

But you didn't *picture* it, right?

There's no need for that, *right?*

Everyone has the same horror of that, and gets there eventually. You have to hope this blown-out version of yourself arrives gracefully, and you let it in the door as if it were an old but not especially interesting friend.

The *future*, though, as Rhodes was trying to conceive it, wasn't that. That picture, and both versions—the old loony bin worker and the venerable pedagogue—were on the other side of some wall. He could sense the wall's trembling presence, as if it were a substance he could plunge through at any second. The decision itself, choosing the path, maybe that was on the near side of the wall. In that sense the future as a real thing and a medium in which he existed, was already here, and he belonged to it. The horrid visions of himself in thirty years, well they belonged to a future, but it was the nominal, abstract future. Living up against the timorous wall, that was the feeling of being alive, of the future's being alive.

All this was catalyzed by Fowler, on the six o'clock smoke. Rhodes, having given out the ciggies, was tipped back against a divider between windows, with the instant coffee he had shielded from Billy Beans. A normal day. Fowler, typically, was in the smoking area; though there was never any eye contact, he preferred to be where the action was, where there was a concentration of PHWs.

"The future," Fowler had led with, looking over the baseball diamonds in the distance, "is not clear. But the wall is. And the funny thing, the recherché and odd thing of it is, I know I can get through the wall. It is like…quartz. It's as hard as anything. But translucent. That's the key. Or the key, my hapless young professional, the key is the fissures that show all through it. I know I can get through.

"Let me share with you my preoccupation: the future which is on the other side. As clear as my transition is, the actual goal is less so. But it involves some productive activity, I sense a farm-like expanse, hordes of productive people. I see the vile and worthless types being mastered by others, organizers with more…depth of soul. I was going to say more education, but that would be trite. More humanity, more ability to create a productive…situation. A controller, too, someone who conceives and executes. Someone…I sense maybe a name…something like…Anton Farmer.

"Thus, through this man's good will and creative genius, people's lives amount to something. Unlike here. Something happens, the world changes, a future evolves."

Chapter 13

In his dream, Rhodes was down in the tunnels, doing Night Doors. In this somber setting—with the dusty floors, clanking steam pipes, weird dips and turns in the tunnel trajectory—the pervasive dream reality was strong: Sherrill Langdon was on his case, and wanted the chore done quickly. Nonsense, of course, because she never assigned Night Doors, and was gone to another ward by that time of night. Still.

And another presence: he bumbled ahead in the tunnels, not really attending to the doors, just wishing he could, if only a white-shirted apparition hadn't just rounded the corner away from him. Voiceless, Rhodes struggled a bit to keep up, turned several more corners, and finally saw it was Anson Fowler.

Fowler was carrying a briefcase. He was wearing a hockey helmet. Again he scuttled off.

Rhodes called to him from 100 feet away. His voice was weak, and the steam pipes, just then, started booming furiously. The more Rhodes tried to raise his voice, the louder the pipes banged.

And he awoke to see a patient restrained on the floor, partially subdued by the charge aide and the hastily summoned charge nurse (male, extra embarrassment for Rhodes and his dereliction). On the ward he'd been given as overtime, overnight. And where the charge aide, a large calm man in suspenders, had urged him—after a final bed check—to just put his head down and sleep.

The patient was kicking a metal wastebasket in his writhing. BANG! BANG! BANG!

Chapter 14

What next hampered Rhodes's romantic quest was Jungle Jim going high.

Jim was slight, with thinning hair, spectacles a bit like Rhodes's wire rims, the look of a rural post clerk. Meticulous in manner. Sat with legs crossed and hands folded in lap. Never spoke. Wore—of the garb the state provided to the shirtless—the rugged plaid model, and had strangely crisp creases in his pants, as if he actually folded them and pressed them under his mattress like a travelling salesman in an old movie. A veteran aide, in a moment of rare wit, came up with "Jungle" for the quiet, fastidious James Alworthy.

He did have his moments. Or moment: his way of "going high" was to get a bit wound up, to sit straighter, to struggle, it seemed, to come out with one word. Unfortunately, the word was banned on B Ward. A kind of *anxietas tibiarum* would take over and he would cross and re-cross his legs with incredible speed. His fingers would start to move like pincers, and a sound, at first like a toilet plunger—the good kind, with the double fold, not the cheap cup model—would start in his throat. Then the sound would get sharper, drier, like a mouse caught in the glue of one of those Roach Motel things, then higher still, a stuttering click like a very large beetle threatening a love rival.

"C-c-c-…C-c-c-c-c…"

Then an aide's threatening bark, "Jim! Knock it off! *Jungle*! You know the policy on that word!" And James would fold up, quietly, like a very fine 19th century toilet kit, and be silent for a month.

Sherrill had just been leaving the ward, Rhodes matching her brisk stride and hoping to get a word in, when this performance caught the nurse's eye.

"Hey! Watch that word, Jim!"

Donny Drouin barking, menacing with pointed finger. Rhodes felt his throat go dry. Sherrill paused for a few seconds before heading for the stairway door—and her gaze rested an extra beat on Drouin. Then she was gone.

Chapter 15

Rhodes wasted his next opportunity as Sherrill skirted his performance with Long John and headed into the nurses' station. The crumpled, two-foot-high package of this man had been given the name Long John in another burst of that irony not at all rare in northern New England, but a bit scarce on the wards. Looking at Sherrill's widening eyes, Rhodes realized that (John needing no medications) she had never seen the man before.

The duty wasn't one of the ones you vied to avoid, like picking up everyone's clothes at night. But you had to watch it. John—whose primitive chart showed absolutely nothing but did indicate, on one faded page, the IQ of a nine month old—had the one skill, the biting-chunks-of-flesh-out-of-you skill, that you really had to watch. Normally he sat in a ball in the same spot in the TV area. He did what you wanted, so you just ordered him to go to the bathroom every three hours. He scuttled along, expressionless, very land-crab, but some compulsion alerted him to carelessness. Just before Rhodes's hiring, he'd taken a hunk out of the charge nurse's calf.

So the bathroom trip wasn't the kind of thing you could break away from, hand off to someone else, if you felt a pressing need to ogle the charge nurse and silently beg her to look up from what she was writing in the shift book. And notice how soulful you were. And suddenly ask you about yourself. Or stretch in the insouciant way teenage girls have that…

Rhodes had once or twice seen her in the empty ward where the time-sheet harpies roosted, and she stood apart from them by actually greeting him. "Hi, Harry," without much of an inflection. This time, in a stroke of brilliant luck, he found her alone when he dropped Long John back in his usual spot and swung into the nurses' station.

"Just finishing up here. Hey, Harry, who was that guy just now, the patient who can't walk?"

"Oh, that's L—that's John. John who...can't walk. Now see, that's an example. I'm wondering if you get more information than we do, or what. There's nothing in his chart. I mean absolutely nothing. Is this the right place for him? It's just an example. Of the kind of thing...I'd love to get your th—"

"The charts are it, Harry. In some cases I think Dr. Burns might know the family, know the story, stuff that led up to this, before any clinical notes get made. In the charts." She was as pretty as ever, her small mouth set in a firm declarative way that suggested she took Rhodes seriously. She gave her glossy, black hair a shake as if she thought there should be more to say, but there wasn't.

"I wonder if he was just dropped at the retarded school, er, the 'state school,' as a baby. Like, in the 1940s? Troubling." After a heart-stopping pause, "So, anyway, how about some time—"

"You know what? Let me get a little more set here, get the deal, personnel-wise and...figure out Burns and all the others. I...So, we'll talk. We will." She had stood up before she said this, checked her keys (for some reason nurses didn't attach them to their bodies) and was leaving. Her age seemed to vault from teen past her real age and up to thirty as she spoke.

As she did this she gave Rhodes's wrist a pat. What you might call—and Rhodes did—a consoling pat.

And the turning back, the little wink, the wink that said his was a hand she might not mind holding, over a couple of cheap beers on Main

Street, or up the Indian joint on Merrimack, that said she knew he was a bit distraught, that he was so thoughtful, soulful, in fact, a soulful guy, so sweet to the patients, obviously someone to get to know, that there was, you know, a winsome quality to his goofy good looks, that she knew the minute she met him—

anyway, it just…wasn't…

there.

Chapter 16

It is fitting now that Rhodes, tipped back with his coffee after the four o'clock smokes, gave thought not so much to the future as to the present.

If you're evening shift, depending on your level of engagement, your *present* can be that late morning before work. The time when you're free, you're you, you're creative. And Rhodes liked to think back on his morning and whatever he'd gotten accomplished.

Well, that was the rub, of course. Unless you have a girlfriend, kids, maybe a dog, your present, at least in the hours before coming onto the ward, doesn't amount to much. Sleeping late, check, couple of errands, OK. Housework, nah. That's about it. The four mornings he ran upstate to teach at Daniel Webster were immensely fun to look back on, from the perspective of the ward. Days like today, though, Wednesday, not so much.

So his thoughts—you'd have to say this was a healthy development—drifted to a different present. He was really present on the ward, and more so every day. For the first time he felt he was getting really good at the job. Which patients to deftly avoid as they stroked and wheedled and tried to shake hands when he came on shift. Which ones to check immediately, and how—based on track record as well as the last few days—to keep tabs on their volatility. How to get a more reflective tone going in his chart notes. When to summon that burst of energy and goodwill, after hours of inactivity, to volunteer for a fairly disgusting chore. He'd been getting a few compliments. Hedged ones from Van. Plumper ones from some older nurses, a surge of these after the time he danced with Billy Beans, masking his discomfort with Billy's bug-eyes and corpse-like pallor, at the make-your-own-ice-cream bash.

But here again our young hero finds himself stymied. There was all that to feel good about. And no comparisons, for the moment, with the more grueling version of fun up at the prep school. And there was his luck in landing on this effervescent ward—could have been the Medical Building, the geriatrics, the warehouse back wards, the "shit wards" (yes, that's why they're called that), the open wards whose tenants wandered the leafy grounds until time for Night Doors. The criminal division. Yet there was something…something he was having trouble putting his finger on…

The fact is that it was nothing complicated or subtle, but he couldn't marshal his thoughts because Davey Doucette was going high. Now, the first few days of this ride, with the Great Entertainer, were fine for everyone. A manic-depressive, a hopeless psychotic, his swings were legendary, but boy, were they fun at the beginning. Right now he was pawing Rhodes's arm, threatening his precious equilibrium in the tipped-back ward chair, and firing off puns, riddles, one liners at an astounding rate. It was Robin Williams before you knew Williams had mental health problems. Well, OK, after you knew. Rhodes knew, but he couldn't help laughing.

"What do you get when you cross a— and a—?"

"Knock knock…"

"Here's my impression of Dr. Burns taking a shit…"

"There was a psychiatrist, a nurse, and a lunatic in a rowboat…"

Material produced at this rate, by a guy who'd been locked up for twenty years and who'd been (charitably put) home-schooled before that—it couldn't all be winners. But he sold it, he had Rhodes laughing, he brought it home with the fantastic energy of his compact body, his soaring voice and deep brown eyes. All the while laughing at his own jokes and repeating, "Harry, Harry…" and pawing away. Peeling off from one audience, he'd sashay down the ward looking for another, with a kind of jazz-hands dance. He'd been known to hop up on the table in the smoking area and do a self-mocking go-go dance. Exertion that left you spellbound.

When he moved off, Rhodes returned to the problem with new clarity. Right. The "being good at the job" somehow itself contained the nugget of doubt. Being good at it up at Daniel Webster almost automatically meant having some fun *and* you had an end result: kids learned something. In the Stack you might have some fun, as with Davey, you might even feel good about being a touch kinder than the average PHW. Yet, Davey might be up one day, then down the next, along with quite a few patients; the cycle was doomed to be repeated, barely commented by the professionals.

And repeated, as Rhodes visualized it, his thoughts again veering sickeningly to the future, decade after decade

So really, what was he doing there?

Chapter 17

As May rounded toward June, Rhodes was still burrowing deeper into his discontent and puzzlement about hospital procedure. In a hazy way, he thought this kind of exercise might lead to a meaningful conversation, one that would advance his cause. A conversation with either Burns or Sherrill.

He started by making lists. The first was a vocabulary list, and he caught himself wondering about this language-teacher approach to things. With "word salad," though descriptive enough of what came out of the Wild Man of Borneo's mouth, he thought they could have done better. "Going high" seemed a little broad; what in the world did Davey's antics, or crushing someone's skull with a cribbage board, or a burst of compulsivity, or biting a dumpling's worth of flesh out of somebody, or the more or less permanent raving of the Wild Man have in common? Likewise "acting out," less grave on a sliding scale as to actual work or punitive action required by staff, seemed only to mean "not immediately doing what you're told." Being "inappropriate" was perhaps the worst. Lower still on the scale in terms of actual usage, though it obviously included high-end stuff like stripping down in front of the nurse, it seemed a needlessly long word to bop patients over the head with. They quickly got the hang of it, mouthing "I been 'ppropriate" when they wanted something. But what did they think it really meant? And, given the wild range of savage, exotic, and illegal manoeuvers seen every day on the ward, it seemed a little niggling.

Worse, the philosopher in Rhodes opined, it was a relative term. While the patients needn't ponder this relativity they sure as hell were subject to it: relative to their situation on the crisis ward of a loony bin, why were so many little things deemed "inappropriate"?

In the perfectly professional lexicon, that is, the notes by actual doctors, the reference "Schizophrenia—undifferentiated type," was especially unhelpful. That was a thing, a real code of some kind?

In another category, the unauthorized category, there was "reality therapy." This generally referred to unapproved Behavior Modification (this wasn't a B Mod ward), such as denying smokes, locking patients up without sign-off from the charge nurse, same drill (if she was off the ward for good) with the bolted chair. A variant of this was "knuckle therapy," though Rhodes had only heard Drouin use the term. He'd seen this PHW—always smiling but with darting eyes, edgy around the patients—fly over the Dutch door as if fitted with a jet pack and land six incredibly rapid punches because a patient had come up to the door and said something innocuous like "Whyncha go fuck yisself."

"Quiet and cooperative," of course, made the list.

"Institutionalized," also, with all kinds of footnotes about how, OK, it was a real thing, but was always said pejoratively. As if unaware of the patient's innocence in this—because, well, who *wouldn't* eventually prefer to stay at the institution and avoid life's challenges after being *forced* to stay there for decades and lose touch with life.

"Religious ideation" seemed as though it could apply to about eighty percent of humanity. But of course it was meant to denote obsessive and oppressive "systems of thought" all based on religion. Fairly common on that campus.

Then Rhodes started another little compendium: the guy who swallowed a toothbrush and had to be cut open vertically, "emergency-style" as someone explained; the guy who lost his finger in a door while holding onto it and fighting with aides; the fragile-looking guy who threw himself down an elevator shaft, twice; the one who kept sticking his thumb up his rectum and then trying to pry out his eye with it; the one who did something imponderable to his member with a pop-top (if the Gentle Reader remembers those sharp things from soda cans in the '60s and '70s); the way Iggy's staph infection was written off as "chronic"; a former B Ward all-star who had bitten off a PHW's nose and had his teeth pulled in retribution; another all-star of old who could only be subdued—and then, barely—by getting him in a headlock and using the free hand to repeatedly slam a heavy door on his skull (according to Dick Knight, who'd seen it done); "Footsie" Beale (Rhodes wished he'd known him better—he left two days after Rhodes's arrival) who stuffed his pillowcase with thousands of pictures of feet, obsessed-over feet torn from mags, comics, ads of all types. These were "behaviors" (this plural, Rhodes thought, should land the word on the other list) which in some cases combined with staff malfeasance, but in any case raised questions. Or more like a foggy process of questioning, for the PHW in question, and a nagging feeling that he needed to get to the bottom of something.

He didn't want to go to Burns with anything open-ended, ill-formed, much less something that sounded like a complaint. He was too new at this, right?

Right?

On the other hand, his deeply concerned floundering might just be the ticket for Sherrill. All at the same time she'd be forced to help him and she'd also see what a sterling character he had. So Sherrill it was.

Just as he said this to himself, the questions partly—but not so much that he didn't still need several alcohol-fueled hours of her help—resolved themselves. One of the questions could be put succinctly: did these "behaviors" occur in spite of the hospital setting (drugs, various professional attentions, inane routines) or *because of it?* For the first time, he felt, with a little shiver, that he ought to watch how he expressed himself around the place.

Chapter 18

Just a quick note about Rhodes's progress with the ward skills. While we're speaking of such things. Such things as his skill with the restraints key. The strange little sliver, like a flattened toothpick, or a gum-stimulator. Releasing restraints on a psychically exhausted patient was not the issue. Rather, it was quickness and dexterity in locking down the portion—an arm, for example—you'd been allotted on a 250-pounder at full chat. Rhodes was slick, springing back with hands wide, the gesture of a calf-roper in a rodeo.

Here, we're focusing on Riot Bell. The way the pros got down to A Ward in about five seconds. The first time the loud buzzer went off, Rhodes, let's just say, brought up the rear, having no idea of the velocity involved. It later seemed like flying to him; you had no idea how you got there, around the bend in the stairwell, many steps at a time, lightning key work at both ends. Soon he was airborne like the rest of them.

And alert.

He worked overtime once on a ward that had a disused old box high on the wall. It had windows that showed which ward to run to on the Bell. But in the present case, it was always A Ward, the women's crisis unit. You had to expect—as happened once, authored by Big Mary—that a heavy oak chair could be streaking through the air toward the door as you opened it. You had, generally, to look out for two others.

Monica, who went high by lowering her head and running it with good speed into a basin or bathroom stall. If she had ever looked like somebody she didn't anymore, her face a lop-sided blend of anxiety and googly-eyed religious sincerity. Orbs both watery and unfocused, leaving no doubt that she saw the world through a numinous haze.

Then there was Zeezie, A Ward's version of Long John, minus any irony, and scuttling like him but equipped with super-speed, able to leap over chairs and tables and escape any but the youngest PHWs, and spraying excrement all the while like a howler monkey.

Big Mary, frizzy and moon-faced, from up north and looking the part, never wearing anything but overalls, could be trouble. There were rare wrestling successes with her. Cajoling, controlling the thrown objects, mopping up the damage were the order of the day. She was a florid psychotic, in the Wild Man's league. Her "word salad" had been tossed and seasoned by a most capricious chef indeed.

All in a day's work for the intrepid Harrison Rhodes—who, after long years of school and odd jobs, was beginning to see what it meant to be a pro. Though a minor slip-up was soon to blot his copybook.

Chapter 19

Rhodes screwed the pooch on the same day that Nurse Langdon struck twice.

He'd been briefed on Zephyr Beauchemin, but had a momentary lapse. Zephyr—a Canadian who didn't speak English, or French for that matter except an occasional "*maudit tabernac*," with an *inappropriate* grin—had a compulsion about windows. If he could get at one he'd break it. As a side note, his breath smelled just a bit like a dumpster on pick-up day. Rhodes had started calling him "Sweetbreeze" (not to his face) and was flattered by imitation.

Sherrill struck by ordering the evening shift out into the courtyard. This hadn't been tried, with B Ward, for years. The fifteen foot, nineteenth century walls were prison-like and made the enclosure gloomy. A tree shivered in one corner; someone had decided it was impossible to shinny up and escape that way. The day wasn't too hot, and Sherrill thought she might overcome the inertia of Rhodes's crew. And of Van, with whom tensions had been building.

The charge aide was, of course, the one most likely to be uptight about a new routine and something going wrong. Understandable enough. It later turned out that, once you got there, through a door off the A Ward stairwell, the patients just stared at the ground and were largely immobile. But you had to bring them all, since there weren't enough PHWs to split between yard and ward. This, of course, raised the ante a bit.

Van opened with, "You have no idea what kind of thing could happen." Face going even pinker than usual, a rigidity seizing mind and body.

Sherrill, going pro herself, showing she'd thought this through, countered with, "Oh like what? It's not hot out, it's a nice day. You could get hurt more easily on the ward. There's just picnic tables down there. And fresh air."

Rhodes admired the combative stance her petite form settled easily into.

"This is a crisis ward. We don't take chances."

"Oh, but you used to. I found out."

"You found out?" This was an unusual Van, a slightly rattled one.

"Yes. I asked around, for heaven's sake. *And* I got Minnie's approval."

"Just like that."

"Van, you can see it wasn't 'just like that.' I put some thought into it, OK? Look, you run a tight ship, you do a good job. But did you ever think we might have fewer crisises" (this high schoolish plural made Rhodes want to jump up and kiss her) "if the patients got more recreation? Or at least got outside?"

Silence all around. None of the staff really wanted the extra work of rounding everyone up, managing an always tricky transition. "So, anyway, let's get it done after smokes—that's almost an hour they can have, before meds."

The fly in the ointment of her victory was Rhodes, whom Van had told, almost in passing, "Harry, you're on Sweetbreeze, OK?" Rhodes, with all the distractions and the change of routine, had barely registered what that meant. He went down the stairwell next to Zephyr, who, seeing the unscreened windows, popped one in an emotionless flash. So Rhodes has to run back for the first aid kit, Van is somewhat vindicated, and the progress in showing Sherrill what a stalwart young PHW one is, what a deep and sensitive...what a...well, that has abated somewhat.

The second way she struck came as Rhodes was doing charts at the end of what had turned out to be a sweaty, tension-filled shift. He took more than his share, knowing full well he was in the doghouse. Van, watching him, coolly and professionally reminded him to do Zephyr's chart. "I did the Incident Report. But you do the notes. You don't put 'due to staff inattention' either—it was due to his compulsion. These things happen."

It was when Rhodes turned to the one mote of pleasure in his evening, the chance to do a good job with Anson Fowler's chart, that it happened.

He turned to the current page and it fell open upon a letter. A sealed envelope with his name on it in a neat and (he later thought) super-feminine hand.

This he opened, using the chart to shield him:

Harry, it would have to be a day we both have off. Obviously. I checked the time-sheet and next Friday could work. Can we grab a beer downtown? I just need to unwind a bit.
Let me know.
—Sherrill.

And suddenly the evening was cool and smooth. The lights were low on the ward, the patients were in bed, work was done, closure on the Zephyr incident. After he read the note fifteen times, only a few little splinters inserted themselves into his thin skin: that she'd written this before she knew of his huge screw-up; the over-specificity of the "grab a beer downtown" as a kind of governor on the evening's soaring, and a limiter of all the probing... the explaining... the complimenting that he'd...er...; the over-explanatory "I just need to unwind," circumscribing it in a different way.

We must believe that, over the next six days, he played out that evening fifty ways and, expert Psychiatric Health Worker that he was, winkled the splinters out one by one.

Chapter 20

In another courtyard session, Rhodes, a little bored and having no fan, newspaper, or other comforts of the nurses' station, sat near Fowler, hoping for some chat. But Fowler just stared at the high wall, perplexed, almost angry. It seemed an inadequate screen on which to project what he more and more often called "the future."

It was different in the smoking room. Rhodes liked that duty. He liked having almost the whole population in front of him—a different density and a tastier kind of tension on hand. And he liked the smell of tobacco, was fighting its lure, even—a nostalgia for his happy childhood which had had, nonetheless, the tang of whiskey in the air along with a blue strato-nimbus of Lucky Strikes. Fowler had figured this bit about Rhodes.

And so he stood, at first with hands clasped behind back, later, as his vision blossomed, with his fingers snaking into the window screen mesh.

"The future, as I think you've heard me say, is not to be understood as a linear progression from the present, or *after* the present. It's more of an inversion, coexistent, a flip that is always available to us. Or an inside-out inversion, sudden, total. That's very apt, you see: the inside becomes outside; the people inside *here*, they are suddenly outside. My wall, the separator, which I see more and more clearly, has quartz-like veins, fissures I've no doubt elaborated. They appear to me more and

59

more heuristic, beckoning almost. The future is palpably *susceptible*. Its presence makes me shiver.

"As to its properties, ah, much to say. These become clearer and clearer. I…perceive, is the right word," gazing far beyond the broad campus, beyond the baseball diamonds at its eastern edge, to a cornfield, "a kind of agrarian community. I see great productivity. All of it outdoors. Great expanses squirming with useful labor. Very intense labor, yes, it is of a farming nature."

Here he drifted off in thought, causing Rhodes to tip his chair forward, start to rise.

"A great stretch of sky, greenish, for some reason. And, in a way that makes my fingers twitch, it is so present—thousands of furrows of a red, laterite earth. Or something like earth. A substance that is the medium of production, of accomplishment, and of something… else…Yes, that's it, I sense it—of a kind of retribution. The rich medium of recompense, retribution.

"Ah, the inversion trembles all around us, it is so feasible, so imminent."

"Er…" Rhodes ventured.

"And you might like to know the very interesting place this inversion will assign you! Not just you. Everyone. Inside-outside. Upside-down.

"The roles you will be assigned!…"

That's a yes—Rhodes was a bit curious.

And, in time, they were assigned.

Chapter 21

When she was only ten minutes late, Rhodes was saying to himself, well, more time to settle in, couple deep breaths, and so on.

When she was twenty minutes late, he gave himself over to wondering. Because she's wicked young? Because she's just wicked, in a selfish way? Or because she's his boss and he's almost beneath her notice?

The Alibi, a good safe choice, not a dive, not loud, and food—if things…developed that way. But not pretentious food. Or anything that might seem like date food. Pine paneling, a lame jukebox, booths in red vinyl. A bartender who looked like a lean serial-murderer-grown-up- version of a child actor, but which one Rhodes couldn't place.

When she dumped her bag on the bar, all was well, except her puff of exasperation.

"Whoa, easy there, Nurse Langdon—as bad as all that?"

"Naw, I just had a bunch of errands. Tough time parking. Phew," flapping her shirt in and out in a charmingly uncouth way, "nice and hot out there."

"I like this place for…" Rhodes fibbed, as if he were a regular, "the lack of certain things, plus good AC."

"Fuckizzat?" with an almost petulant nod at our hero's beer.

He vouchsafed, after the briefest pause, "I'm enjoying a nice glass of porter, since you ask."

"Porter?"

Now, this was flat out entrancing, revealing once again her age (later revealed to be twenty-one). Her crude ways, well, Rhodes would manage to find them beguiling too.

In truth, he'd been hung up for twenty minutes or so on the horns of his various binary propositions. Barnes or Burns, Teacher or Back Ward Wrestler? An attack on the way the institution cared for certain patients, yes, but initiated through Burns or through Sherrill? As to her, a full-on attack on the sovereignty of her body or, putting that aside for a bit, an investigation of her mind, *in re* the patient problem?

"Porter is some kind of ale. Some people say it's a blend, a blend of…I like it because—"

"I'll have a Coors," she told the serial murderer. She said it the local way, that sounded something like *caws.*

"Want to get a table?"

"Sure," with a slack mouth, but a little more smile in the eye area.

Once seated, in a near-panic about what to say, Rhodes suddenly pitched forward, grinding his sternum against the table. "I've been dying to ask you. Why did you go into psych nursing instead of, you know, up the city hospital or somewhere?"

"Oh, I don't know," blowing a raven's wing of hair out of her face. "It was an opening. I did think it would be interesting. I took a lot of psych courses."

"Right. Me too. Everyone did." A smile to soften this.

She laughed. "Well, right. But they don't prepare you for *this*. And it *is* interesting. And you do some medical stuff, you know. I catheterized a guy the other day." Rhodes winced. She didn't notice. "And you see some heinous wounds."

"That you do." Again plunging forward, "But here's the thing. I mean, wouldn't the whole job be better, and more interesting, if diagnostics, treatment plans, access to records—I don't know—all that, weren't so casual? If you really got interested, how much could you learn about a patient?" He sat back, amazed, and thus, suddenly pleased, that there was no more to it, he'd said it the way he'd meant to.

Her half-closed, slightly evasive eyes didn't change, but she stopped fidgeting around and looked at Rhodes in a way that added six or eight years to her age. And kept it up. "I know. I mean, yes, and I know what you mean. I heard you the first time, about that, on the ward. I put some time into it. Kinda curious myself, and all."

After a moment's appraisal—Rhodes was pretty sure it was of him— she went on, "I'll tell you what I did. I went to Burns on, like, a pretense. Pretext, whatever. I said, 'Hey I've been wondering about Medication Reviews, on some individuals. And in general. Like, when were the last ones done? I can help out. If you let me look through some records I could get the ball rolling, if it needs to be done in a big way. The records are mostly in here, right? I could divide it up, do a few every day. Like, whaddya say,' kind of thing, right. He just stares at me. 'Yes the… files are here. Yes I have files. Of course I have files,' he goes. That's all he says. Calls me 'Carol' or something. Then he just turns his back on me, 'I'll let you know. I'm busy.' I wondered why he kept calling them 'files'."

"I think I know why."

"Anyway, there's always Minnie Jewel, and she's great, and I do mean to sit down with her. She's doing a performance review of me, but that's a few weeks off."

"So we're behind the importunate eight-ball." Her eyes narrowed slightly. He went on, clinking her glass with his, "This might require multiple sessions, much strategizing!" Her smile, a bit sidelong before a massive slug of Coors, encouraged him. "I mean, there must be a way around this. What if, for example, Minnie is totally respectful of our young enthusiasm and so on, and has—a long shot—a key to his office? Or duplicate 'files'? Or what if there's another way to show we want to improve treatment, set up a program for one patient, let's say, and we set the thing in motion, the day shift aides are following along, we're getting praise for it, and *then* we say we need access to a little more background information."

"OK, I follow. The long game."

"Yes, sadly protracted as a stratagem. But," and here the second porter was asserting itself, and Rhodes plunged ahead heedless of whether his emphasis came from the solid, effective planning or from the excitement of roping her in, "the beauty is we would do good work in the meantime. Even if we're treated like yokels, denied the intellectual satisf—I mean, unable to really learn or put deep thought into a patient's diagnosis and all, we'd be making common sense improvements in their treatment. Not just 'treatment program,' right, but how they're treated, treated as humans, every day."

"Huh."

"Right? We got this, this is doable!"

"Harry, you're too much. I mean, yes. Yes, I'm with you. I'm trying to make that clear. I'm just looking at you wondering when you're going to burn out."

"Hah!"

"You burn out after we've done all this work, become like your buddies. All the people around here."

"OK, what's that, *your* burnt-out tone I'm hearing? Is that what I'm hearing? We're both pretty new, so…So now's the time, right?" This with a big ol' smile, trying to lighten everything up. "You want another canister of fizzy water?" Another attempt.

Both attempts worked, or else it was a fat woman punching a wizened little man in the shoulder, back at the bar, with less and less friendliness in the slab of her face. Sherrill settled what looked like a professional gaze on her. "Yeah, I'll have one more."

Rhodes brilliantly, as he later thought, kept the chit-chat light after that, focusing on the town, the summer around the corner, a couple of great movies. He also (brilliant? chickenshit?) kept it off her, her personal life, his interest.

She left after an hour and a half. He left after four drinks.

And, a few hours later, exiting with the fat woman's voice fading behind him ("The *fuck it is!* The *fuck it is!*"), he realized that, aside from the burn-out bit, Sherrill hadn't asked him one thing about himself.

Chapter 22

"These whoresons! These curs!" (Fowler again, with a good head of steam up.) "Lick-spittles of the dark bureaucracy! Oh, the higher their pinnacle of power the more will they soon wallow. Dr. Cartwheels" (Cartwright), "Professor Simperings" (Simpson), "Superintendent Pee-Stains" (Perlstein). "What a barnyard of benighted livestock, what swine."

"Say, Anson, did you…did you happen to just have an appointment with Burns?"

"These purblind denizens of the endless syoo-wer, the pipestream of psycho cacophony. These eels!" The pose by the window was the same, but his body was rigid, his eyes seemed fixed on the screen instead of the hazy distance. He trembled slightly. "Yes. I saw the tired old whore. I was dragged before him, strapped down, subjected to…subjected to…" Now, body and gaze seemed to relax very slightly, as if with weariness.

"You know, I did say I'd talk to him about you, so I will. I'm going to make an appointment. I had some reasons to put it off, after I forgot that time. But let's get after it. I hope that helps—I'm promising."

Rhodes had to leave the area and admonish Jungle Jim. Looking back, he saw that Fowler was absolutely motionless.

"C-c-c-cu-cu!"

"Jim! James! Knock it off!" Quick compliance, quick work. Rhodes thought that, as long as he was up and about, he should peek down the leg of the ward invisible from the smoking area. He walked a few steps and ran right into Dr. Burns.

This authority figure, like a bookend to Fowler, a bulbous bookend, stood with his hands hooked behind his back and face empty of expression, before a window. The window was the small plexiglass viewer in the Wild Man's door.

"Spect-ocular spect-ocular!" in the Wild One's idiom, "Won't you come in? The walls have come in, that they have that they have that they have. On the other hand the diamonds are encrusted with baseball players. Entrusted with prayers. Such a long story. I'm sure we have time."

Looking with difficulty past Burns's head, Rhodes could see the patient's typical wide eyes, somewhat tense posture, yet openness, an almost affable invitation to talk, and a kind of deep eye contact. It was an expression he liked, and the whole package was known to be trouble free, on the escorts to the bathroom, except that you had to wade in the stream of consciousness. Listening was always eerie, and Rhodes was more than a little disturbed when he turned to see Burns's reaction.

There was no sign of life, no human response. It was like the face of a drowsy cow—maybe one that was dimly aware of a fly about to land. Wild Man went on, and the Burns non-reaction became more and more troubling.

"Who's to blame? It's all the same. Name of the game. The game of the blame. A walk would be fine, spank you. Just in time. *That's* what I've been talking about! Do you follow? Does he follow? A *stroll* in time. The time is ample, come in and see!"

"Dr. Burns," Rhodes very quietly interjected.

"Time is a sample! Everything's free!"

Burns glanced at the PHW in a way that showed he hadn't been half-asleep, and this made his blandness somehow more offensive. "Yes? Oh, it's you."

"I'd like to make an appointment with you."

"Oh! Fine. Excellent. Just do it, just call the extension, they'll set it up."

Well, two things.

One: that Burns answered with alacrity but didn't ask what was up portended that he had more of his own murky designs to prosecute.

Secondly: if he had so slight a reaction to his most psychotic patient, then why was he visiting him in the first place? He left without speaking to the poor young man. The whole thing had a way of suggesting the outside world. It suggested something of Wild Man's outside life— Rhodes knew it to be middle class, fairly educated—and that someone had asked Burns to do more with this patient. And that's the only reason he'd made a rare visit to the ward.

Chapter 23

June continued to pound home the truth of summer—that the old wards get hotter as the evening wears on.

PHWs were sprawled in the station, all the charts done, wordless. The usual crew, minus Galt, Dick Knight filling in. Rhodes had been looking at the ceiling, listening to the awful whisper of the Stack, its occasional descant. Suddenly, as if many of his quandaries, many of his opaque binaries, many of the unanswerables of life in his late twenties had all at once decided to land on his head and sink their claws in like vicious…sink their…like…like…—he lurched forward.

"Fellas. Listen, what's this sound like, for an idea: we become the Action Heroes of B Ward, we liberate some of these zombies from the wordless anomie, the weird suspension we've put them in, the lack of…What if we tried to do it, one at a time. Say, we choose one patient, we study up, get some of the gung-ho types on day shift involved—"

"What…?"

"What are you…?"

"Aw, come on…"

"What's anomie?"

"Faggot."

"No, listen. We get the higher-ups involved too, we look like champs. We make it clear the actual 'treatment plan' isn't doing anything, we just sort of call for a review. We draw something up together. Concrete. Better recreation. One-on-one time. Maybe behavior mod. Whatever."

"What the fuck is wrong with you?" This last from Drouin.

A mere chuckle from Van, who then held up his hand, "OK, guys, OK, let him finish."

Rhodes swallowed hard, not having thought all of this out, and having only tenuous buy-in from Sherrill. "We could just do it one at a time. Of course. Or just *try* one. Try Moose, or Anson, for example. Fowler."

"Rant-son?" Drouin again. "What's there to do? He's an open book. Crazy as a bedbug, and high functioning, and plus probably likes it here. Case closed. Next. Oh, Billy Beans? Great—try having a conversation with him. What the fuck are you thinking?" Here he started making the only noise anyone had ever heard out of Billy, cupping hand over mouth and then releasing, "Boo-WAH!"

"OK, just lemme finish."

"Let Florence Nightingale finish over there."

"Thanks, Dick. Maybe you actually care, I can never tell with you…"

"Boo-WAH! Boo-WAH!"

"Oh I care, Rhodesie. I care with a growing passion in my left nut *that it's 10:48.*"

"OK, fine. All I'm saying is…You know what, there's another way to look at this: we're all in danger of turning into zombies ourselves, d'you ever think of that? That's kind of what's happening here, I mean. If we don't do anything, and the society we're in, locked in, is *this,*" waving his hand out toward the ward as watches were glanced at and knapsacks started to get packed up—business eerily similar to the last minute of class, up at the prep school—"our fate is kind of linked to—"

"That's it!" As the first night shift PHW swung in, dropped his bag. "Rhodesie," Knight went on, "we get *paid* to be zombies. That's the beauty of it. You're missing the essential beauty of this line of employment. *God.* I wonder about you sometimes."

Rhodes knew Van had to stay to read out the shift book to the next bunch, so he stood, gave him kind of a hopeless look. Van, in the end, would play this one whichever way the wind blew. For now, his smile was fairly kind. "Harry, you got it out, you said it about as well as could be." After a long reflection, which was either about the profundity of Rhodes's ideas or about the simplest way to shoot him down, he went on, "You'd just have to figure out a way to put it that doesn't sound like *work.*"

Chapter 24

As Rhodes stepped like a blind man into the turbid office of Dr. Burns, he reminded the august physician, "Dr. Burns, I have an app—"

"Yesyes. Yesyesyesyes!" The fish behind him, in response either to his peevish tone or to the young PHW's blocking the light from the door, skirted a miniature diving bell and darted into a cave.

"This isn't a probationary check, right—just reminding you. What I really wanted to—"

"Any time! Doesn't matter. Been wanting to talk to you. Now," patently ignoring whatever Rhodes had come for, "this business of your brilliant career. Heh. Your psych career. Fascinating field, as you've no doubt discovered. *Or,* taking another branch entirely, in the *guh*...oo-woad of life, your miserable, overworked, groveling, threadbare, and increasingly neurotic life as a schoolmaster—a life that verges on murderous psychosis every year at contract-signing time—in a fetid little dump for damaged and cast-off children. Sure. Great. Let's have a little discussion of all that, the pros and—"

"Well, but. I mean, yes, for a moment—lots to decide, but I haven't really dec—"

"Dammit man!" A hand like a marked-down package of hamburger, the 70% lean, slammed on the desk. A little more light in the two eye-slits. "They're doing contracts up there now, aren't they? Done, for most people? You haven't decided, you can't decide? He must be all over you, as *guh...*" (the brief panic perceptible in the dark) "oo-wepulsive as that—"

"Oh, I'm in a special situation."

"Hah!"

"With, you know, not being full-time. Plus he's not sure he has four Latin classes to give me. Still working that through with the language folks up there. This guy LaLumière, the temporary Chair up there. It might come down to my teaching English or something. Too."

Long pause.

"Uh huh. Listen to yourself. And then Latin bombs after a couple of years, and we all know how hard English teachers are to find—*guh...*oo-woadkill is too elevated a term for what you'll be after Barnes drives over you with his big, fat, his monstrous..."

"Right. Of course. That's what I'm weighing. So I do need a little more time..."

Burns showed himself capable of absorbing a few new facts, and reflecting on them. "So... this means they're even more keen on you than I thought. A problem...What do I have to do? I have a certain vision of the ward, as I think you know, I'm trying to—"

"Right, I got that. Last time. Really, I'm super interested in that, the job is great. I'm lucky to be on B Ward. Here's the thing, though, if we could postpone the...deciding problem...just postpone—"

"You know that after summer there might not even be a position for you here, unless you move into Career Stairs?"

"Yes, that crossed my mind. But, for now, what I came to see you about—"

"GOOD CHRIST, MAN!" At this the diving bell shivered, threatened to tip over.

"But let me explain..."

"You do that thing. You explain to me. What I don't know." This imperative was softened by his slight gasp as he tried to find a new

73

position in his chair—alas, only one position was possible—and by the fish's comically tentative appearance behind his left elbow.

"OK, so, a couple of us have been thinking, we might actually tune up our approach to some of these patients, find a way to give them a little more...well, more of everything. Interactions, recreation, thoughtful charting, diagnostic review..." (here an excuse-me kind of cough) "that kind of thing. Wondering how long it's been—"

"How long it's been since I exercised my actual profession on that type of thing, is that what has you up at night—"

"Oh gosh, no—what I mean, the novelty of the thing is...we were thinking of a new kind of team. Get PHWs and nurses, and Minnie, you of course," (cough) "different shifts all putting their heads together. A new kind of experience for us, and would probably generate some—"

"OK OK OK. Stop."

A very long pause, in which Rhodes decided that the doctor's gaze at the ceiling was a tad theatrical.

"Let me er, *generate* for you the vision which I had hoped would stick the first time."

And what followed, with references to "college" and "degree," cast a dizzying spell over our young hero. What, his B.A. was so richly prized by this maniac, Rhodes having carefully scraped his Master's degree off his hospital c.v.? While his M.A. was merely adequate up north at the school? What was the bottom line of this little editorial on his life-choices? Was this juxtaposition some sort of guidepost? This way: yearly extortions and humiliations by the fat monster Barnes? That way: being a kind of window-dressing in the fantasy of the fat monster Burns?

"I think I've made clear, *guh*... er, Harrison, that I need to kick this place up a notch. You would, of course, be a PHW 2, then, taking your cues from me, in *guh*...oo-wapid succession, charge aide and then charge aide on the day shift. As such, a person who actually does work with Minnie, who actually influences ward policy. Er, to some degree."

Rhodes got it, along with the abrupt truth that his original subject, his purpose in coming, had barely been heard. Was dead. And were these last enticements, as he glanced at his watch, started packing up his scattered psyche to leave, enough to overcome the window-dressing bit?

No. Not as it turned out. "And, as I said last time, my friend, you would add some tone to the place. For example when the fuc—the goddamn legislators come through here. Or, God forbid, the newspapers. I need someone like you standing there, day shift. Eloquent. Politic. Not someone who looks like they just fell out the woodshed window."

Rhodes's fall, as he headed for the ward, was long, tumbling, and dark.

Chapter 25

"In this reversal, this upside-downing, this vast inversion I have outlined to you, the loser now will be later to win type of situation," (here we notice Fowler's tiniest of smirks) "which is so tremulously imminent as to be a future that is present—that is, if the ontological pump, the Soul Pump I have described can be made to reverse, to spew us back into *being*, to spew us forth as *souls* while it sucks in at the other end the vampiric charlatans—I should say *when*, not *if*, this comes to fruition certain conditions will obtain.

"Those who have humbled and regimented our lives will themselves be marched out to the fields where the substance of retribution is tilled. To be thus under the yoke and to be always harvesting is the substance of the substance, if you follow. For the retribution is the work itself, which will be endless.

"Oh, and grueling. Nothing can compare to the horror of this toil. The Roman salt mines are as nothing, the slaves working for Hitler's Krupp are blithe picnickers, the swampy tree-felling of the French prison colonies is as a badminton party, in comparison. There are many reasons for this. But of course the main one is the iron teleology of justice.

"Technical reasons: the substance. Let's call it *humble humus*. The workers, to stay sane in a way that they can stand, that spares them the most nightmarish forms of unbalanced consciousness, have to stay humble. That is the substance of the exercise. And the medium is the humus, which they must toil from the first light seeping over the garish mountains until they are shackled and marched back to their sleep pods. Oh, it is a long and shattering day. But productive. That is, if they have maintained their humility every second. Otherwise, a night of the most hellish, the most searing visitations awaits.

"Should they awake, should they force themselves awake to spare themselves, the wardens—matrons along the lines of the one you call Big Mary—release a jet of gas into the pod that administers sleep once again."

Chapter 26

"Someone as shrewd as you—not shrewd enough to be spared, alas…so sad—will have picked up the hierarchy of the thing. The retribution distribution, hah. Your Ubus, if he can be found, your Pee-Stains, Blisters, Cartwheels, Simperings et al., along with Administrative Head Nurses and charge nurses, will be the serfs.

"Also in a hellishly painful role will be those nominally below them, now above: the psygoads. Regular nurses and PHWs, criminal division aides, adolescent division 'teachers.' For them, the long days, fitful nights in the sleep pods, and inspection of extremities are no different from the serfs' lot. Think of them as rather like the kapos in a concentration camp.

"More on their goading regimen later. But first, a word about the ambience. All takes place under a sky of bilious green, shot through at times by bands of mustardy haze. The nearby hills are an insane hue of orange, while the furrows that stretch to the horizon are bright, rusty red. There is never a breeze. The heat and humidity are a touch above— oh, let's make it considerably above—that of the swamps of French Guiana. There is nothing else, no feature in the landscape; the hills are behind the serfs, and the Controllers are ensconced in them. There is nothing but the furrows. The day's job is to till straight in the furrow, fourteen hours, to reach the horizon. But, of course, horizons being what they are…

"It must be understood that the *humble humus* remains friable and workable only if it is dug up and exposed to air once a day. In this process, as it is flopped in damp humps along each furrow, it turns a deep purple. The next day it must be pushed back, using the hands like ploughshares, into the furrow. It must not be allowed to dry. It lies abed, turns red again, neither too wet nor too dry, and the following day it is dug up again."

Rhodes shifts uneasily, earnestly tries to accept this man's message while also trying to anaesthetize the nastier salients.

Jimmy Galt's voice rings in the ward.

Fowler sighs, "Oh dear, must be seven o'clock. Another dose of Controlemol."

Chapter 27

"The task of the psygoad is to effect the day's retribution, to make sure the work is unrelenting in the fields of justice. In the crawl toward the ever-receding…To make sure that the Controllers' view is utterly pullulating with the bent backs of the serfs, the upright waddle of the goads. Each psygoad urges three or four serfs ahead of him, *or her*, in the furrow. Why is this such punishing work? The goad is not allowed to walk in the furrow. To do so—or at least this is what they're told—would damage the substrate. More to the point, their bare feet would remain stained with red, not purple. To pass inspection at night their feet must be as purple as the serfs' hands. And so they have to straddle the furrow, and shuffle along that way. After an hour or so their thighs are like jelly, another half hour and intense pains shoot through their legs and lower backs. By mid-day their groin muscles are on fire. There is nothing they can do to relieve this agony. Keeping their balance as their feet land in the wet humus and they reach forward awkwardly, oh, so awkwardly, to poke at the serfs with their heavy goads requires the utmost concentration. Their sweat blinds them, their goads are no use for balance in the soggy humus, the workers in the other furrows threaten to pull ahead. It is an awful lot they have, in effect, *chosen.*"

Chapter 28

Rhodes was on his perch where the two legs of the ward joined, the elbow of the L. He watched the Moose advance toward him from one of the far ends.

"Now, see," he lectured himself, "this is a perfect example." Moose was six foot eight, pink of face and grey of crew cut, and solid, walking off all the hot dog buns and Wonder Bread the hospital could feed him in the several miles he paced each day. He never stopped. No one could keep shoes on him either.

Rhodes listened to the soft slap of the bare feet, offered "Hi, Elwin," at the turn to the other wing.

"Hi." This was Moose's only word, but was dropped so naturally, with a sound a bit like "hoy," or "huy," but very clipped, very North Country, that it was easy to imagine that a whole vocabulary, a complete conversation, were possible.

"Here's a guy," the PHW went on, to himself, "whose presence makes no sense here. Unless people are just afraid of him. He's been here forty years, no one ever puts any time into him—and all because, possibly, he hit someone or threw something on another ward, decades ago. You could, for one thing, probably *should*, experiment a little by putting him on another ward."

An idea began to form in the increasingly overwrought mental health worker's brain. Why not use Moose as the Trojan er, horse. Start with Moose as a practicum, a focus for the dream team he was conceiving, the team that would review each patient, see about the necessity of crisis ward placement, do med review, treatment plan review, improvement in relevant daily charting. Maybe Fowler was too daunting. Moose was charted as B.O.S., burnt-out schizophrenic. But those types abounded on other wards. If his psychosis was so burnt-out, was he really a danger to anyone? And what did that mean, beyond the unprofessional but accepted sound of it, except that the warehoused patients were often put in that category and, by a sort of *tradition*, were then considered unworthy of further attention. But wouldn't they, in their burnt-out condition, now be amenable to talking therapy, to drawing them back into life, into real relationships, things they loved and so on? Maybe Rhodes had more to learn about the condition, but these questions were sensible starters for the whole team, if he could get anyone to listen.

Then you would move on from there, in this plan, under a Burns-Sherrill-Minnie Jewel constellation firmly fixed in a perfect 3:00-11:00 sky, to other patients. What were they doing on B Ward? When was the last time anyone evaluated *anything* about them? Of what value was the current style of comment in their daily charting? You moved on: to people like the Wild Man of Borneo, seemingly in permanent crisis, and Anson Fowler, seemingly in better shape mentally than half the staff.

To stir this kind of rumination into an unhealthy froth was the fact that Sherrill had taken a week's vacation, Burns had started taking four-day weekends, and Minnie Jewel was on vacation as well. Rhodes felt adrift, and, to further twang the high-wire between his two jobs, it now occurred to him that summer (with all the vacations) might have been the worst time for him to come to the hospital and to try to see if the job couldn't be changed in a way that competed better with the teaching angle.

Certainly, this was the time to hit the books. The ones he'd rounded up—Szasz, Laing, others—that Jimmy Galt had made passing reference to. The ones that questioned the very idea of mental illness. Had the world dismissed these practitioners as quacks? Was the Stack the one place in the world where their ideas would never catch on? Quite likely. Along with Rhodes's idea that some of the doctoring was a bit like the Heisenberg Uncertainty Principle: if you were focusing on the exact mental state of a patient at one point in time (and the charts seemed to do that! an admission date long in the past!), then you had no knowledge of his movement—toward or away from whatever good mental health was. And if you were looking at what you thought was movement—progress, or regression—then you didn't have one fixed and accurate diagnosis.

Rhodes's head was spinning—at all the implications of this, at the thought of the throngs of patients who could benefit from a new approach. Also at the thought—not new in his life—of bolting, of running from this Uncertainty, just dealing with goofy, lusty, well-favored kids up north.

Ah, but tomorrow! Tomorrow Minnie was back. He could come in fifteen minutes early, before she took report from the day nurses, and try some of this out on her.

Chapter 29

"The Controllers, meanwhile, reside in a glass structure built into the hills, seemingly in perpetual shade, with polarized glass ever soothing to the eyes. They loll in a pleasure dome, a pleasance of unparalleled ease and comfort. They sprawl before the vista of endless furrows in great soft recliners, each equipped with every appurtenance of support. They have little to do. Should inactivity induce the slightest hint of ennui, movies of startling originality, or music and literature of a challenging vivacity are provided. No one is subservient, there are no cooks or maids. They vie with each other in the creation of cunning little *hors d'oeuvres* and cocktails.

"Work, if you can call it that, consists of a scattered few administrative chores during the day. Desultory charts are kept, notes on how different psygoads are doing, how much humility 'progress' is being made out in the fields. Occasionally chastisements have to be seen to, at night.

"It is clear, I hope, that each night is a punishing raft of terror, due to nightmares (more on these later), for the typical worker who passes extremity inspection and falls asleep. We have seen that those who 'have trouble falling asleep' are quickly dealt with. For those, however, whose hands, or feet, are not sufficiently purple, there are other measures. The hue, of course, is a sure sign that a serf has not heaved the proper quantity of muck out of the furrow, or that a goad has chosen to walk in its substrate. For these, there is the 'talking cure.'"

Chapter 30

The next day was a teaching day, so there was an interlude. And before the actual teaching, another break, as Rhodes eased the old Triumph into a parking spot on Wentworth Lane, in front of the academic building. He hadn't been given a parking slot, so he always clambered out of the roadster among a crowd of students running late who viewed both him and the old rig as curiosities.

This time he was a few minutes early and sat reflecting on the idyllic scene before him. Braced against piney hills, the school buildings showed off red brick in finer proportions than those of the hospital, with frou-frou such as granite lintels. The trees were more judiciously placed. Signage somehow had the look of classic literature. Here was an ambiance that whispered (but loud enough to be heard in New York, Connecticut, Maryland): Bring us your bored, your wan, your self-indulgent huddled over expensive playthings. This is the ideal shelter for them while you get your divorce, while they figure out why Bob Dylan is actually more important than Kanye West. While they take a last shot at a so-so college.

Was this a place where Latin needed to be pounded into their heads? Or would all the other chores—Headmaster Barnes had been quite vague about these—that went with being full-time faculty provide interesting challenges for Rhodes, interesting arenas for what's best about kids outside the classroom? For the gambols and misadventures, it dawned on him, that were modelled on his own from just ten years back. Fatally attractive, the whole thing, when looked at that way.

Ach…the pang those memories brought. When he thought (silly man, he didn't think of himself as young) of his teen years. His Barracuda, which he thought was hot even though it only had the Slant Six under the hood, the necking he'd conducted in the leafy lanes of his Eastern Massachusetts home. His presidency of the Classics Club, a few toga parties that fell short of the epic. His bewilderment about college, talks with his earnest parents about it, final acceptance of the idea. The effervescence in his head-bone, freshman year, of such courses as Religion, Cultural Anthropology. The empty miles as he drove a cab, the year between college and grad school.

He never allowed time or occasion, before class, to run into Barnes or be summoned by him. And the Headmaster blew off lunch duty, so Rhodes could wolf the offerings, learn what this kind of "duty" entailed, and then beat it out of town. All went as planned this day, and our young hero was soon motoring down 127, planning out a quick elevator-pitch for Minnie Jewel.

He had to park in a new spot, nearer Minnie's office in the Main Building, and a snarling match with an old-school uniformed nurse delayed his entrance. She had dived for the slot his Triumph had partial possession of—its sprite British stature making it invisible to her.

So Rhodes bounded up the wooden steps—surprisingly rickety for such a massive brick building—two minutes late, double-timed through the warren that led toward the administrative offices. With the half-formed thought that Sherrill's vacation might be over, that she might soon be taking report from the day shift in Minnie's office.

Just Minnie, with her back to the door, gazing over the long slope toward the Geriatric Building. Her office was small, accentuating her height, and it was messy. It was the kind of mess that told of hard work, extra hours plugging the gaps, total integrity. Minnie's hair was black like Sherrill's, but longer. Her head was small and round, not a common thing in this region of long-heads. When she turned around her black eyes twinkled with something Rhodes had forgotten—a kind of witty condescension toward everything. Because it wasn't directed at anyone in particular, it was an enjoyable wit, and a refreshing impression of superior mind.

"Oh, hello, Harrison."

"Hi, I was wondering if you have two minutes?"

"Sure—and how do you like it here so far?" A bit of a smile at her own boldness.

"Oh, fine. The whole thing's fascinating, I'm loving it. Wouldn't take up your time, but. Well, here's the thing."

"Have a seat for God's sake."

"OK, here's the thing. About that. The simplest way to put it is: why are certain people on my ward—originally (sometimes it's in the chart, sometimes not) or why are they *still*—and, don't take this wrong, but, like related, why am I here?"

"Develop."

Her kind eyes were the first invitation of any kind to really go into what was bugging him. Maybe to untangle some of the reading he'd been doing, figure out if Career Stairs was just that, steps for the employee, leading to a door of some kind, a good door for him—but having nothing behind it for the patients.

Had her response registered? He continued, "I mean, even if I wanted to spend more time with certain patients, try to draw them out, pull them back toward something normal in the way of conversation, right, or relating to people…"

"But you *do* want to, yes?"

"Yes. But you have to have something to go on. The charts is…are…a good example. If you don't know much in the way of diagnosis, or you can see it's from fifteen years ago, and no one has

87

made any notes about behavior or plans to shape that—you see what I'm driving at? Someone like Elwin Morrill. I mean, where do you start? Maybe all these big places are like this, or my idea would never work, I don't—"

"My private horror is that all these places operate this way, and that it won't change. Small private places—and you could work in one of those, but don't, don't leave us!—maybe they're different. But *this* is what these patients can afford. Or their families." She was sitting back in her chair, looking at the floor. When she looked at Rhodes he had the feeling she knew something about him no one else did—but then, she always looked like that. He started wondering, suddenly, about her and Burns. Was this one of the things she knew: how much was, or was not, possible at that institution? "Be aware, even more than you are now, of the inertia in this place. Sometimes I think the whole place was built with inertia bricks and no-can-do mortar."

"Well, still I got to thinking there's no reason we couldn't try, as a group, to kick it up a notch. Charting, planning, more frequent reviews. Team meetings. Get the day shift, of course, and you, and—"

She leaned forward in her chair, pinched the bridge of her nose. Then a piercing, but still merry, glance met Rhodes's. "I know all about it, I heard. I know what you're thinking—Sherrill Langdon told me."

Well now. She would have had to tell Minnie more than a week back. What especially goosed Rhodes at this point was that after their session at The Alibi, Sherrill had filled in on other wards, had said nothing to him, and had then gone on vacation. And he'd been more and more uneasy about this. Understandable uneasiness, after what he thought was not only a fun booze-and-chat but also a wee bit of soul-baring. But this little piece of news meant that at least his professional confidences had gotten somewhere with Sherrill. The homerun would be if Minnie, too, was impressed with the plan.

She stood as a day nurse came in. "OK, look, I think it's great, do it, get after it—keep your head down in certain areas. We'll talk. Tell Sherrill we're doing it. Get her thinking."

Bam! Took the fastball right out of the catcher's mitt.

"She's back tomorrow, you know."

The crowd didn't stop cheering till he was well around third base...

Chapter 31

"C-c—c-cu-cu!—"

"Hey! Knock it off! Jim! Jungle," Rhodes losing his cool, "you know about that word!" Jim's eyes were pinballing around in his head, but he crossed his legs, folded his hands, and was quiet.

If life is often comedic, as you may have reckoned—and the life of Rhodes, even if he could sort the Burns and Barnes flamboyance, was bound to be this way in the present setting—it's because it abounds with clownish figures. As he followed Sherrill, somewhat embarrassed, into the nurses' station he thought it would be nice if people could be serious.

Since she stood still, seeming to have no other reason to be there, he started in with his preoccupation. "So guys, that thing I was talking about, improving charts—well, you know, the whole thing, better attention to treatment plan and stuff—let's get on it, OK? Let's be famous, let's make a model team, even a model for how other wards can pick their game up. And so on."

"What…?" A goofy slack jaw from Dick Knight.

"The proposal has been duly considered…" This, with eyes way too close together and a chipmunk mouth, from Filbert.

Jimmy Galt stared hard, with the tiniest smile replacing his usual wide grin.

Sherrill and Van just stared hard. At each other.

Donny Drouin threw himself back in an imitation of Live-Free Lenny, raised one foot off the floor to fart—then, perhaps in deference only to Sherrill's great looks, subsided.

Because the nurse was there, the proposal was not greeted with the guffaws and raspberries of its first roll-out. A measure of silence, palpable uptightness from Van, then Dick who, let's face it, really didn't give a damn about anything, "You mean the 'Pick a psycho and work our asses off improving his life' thing?"

Rhodes countered with, "Well, good, Dick, in a manner of speaking, yes. Good, *Dick*. Not the worst plan of action ever. And it's not like we're not getting *paid*."

Sherrill seemed calmer than Rhodes. With a grin she threw in, "Come on, guys. No problem, right, could be fun. And like Harrison says," ("Harrison? *Harrison?*" amid open hooting from some team members—the full name an unforeseen hurdle) "you'll look good to the bosses and everyone. You *are* getting extra pay for this ward, and what better place to put out a little, than a crisis unit?"

Van, who had been writing in the report book as a way of both releasing his own tension and showing obvious disregard for the proceedings, shut the book and tried to adopt a tone of finality. "Yeah. So. Speaking of the higher-ups, let's just see what Minnie has to say about it. She's not—"

"Minnie's approved it." Van stared at her, bug-eyed. "She wants it to happen." The silence, if silence can increase, increased. Turning and leaving, "I have to pass meds downstairs. Harrison's your man, he's got good ideas." And, with an air that Rhodes thought was maybe a little flippant, "I leave you in his hands."

After a few beats, in a voice dripping with venom, Drouin: "Well now. Well now, college boy..."

Chapter 32

He was increasingly drawn to tunnel work. He volunteered for Night Doors. So much that Drouin noticed, "Like it down there, huh? Doin' anything down there we should know about?"

Van backed him off, "Alright, D.D., let him do the job. He does more work than all of us put together, so…"

"I'll just secure the place, Donny, while you sit up here and scratch your nuts for half an hour, OK?" Rhodes threw over his shoulder.

What was it about the tunnels? Well, for one thing, you weren't surrounded by large numbers of unpredictable insane people. You weren't being observed by your superiors. You didn't have to work alongside your rough and tumble PHW crew. And it was cool.

Just had to be alert. A bit like a cop or night watchman on a solo beat. Bark with authority. And so Rhodes paused at a certain corner, before rounding into sight. Yep, the predicted slurping, the time-tested rhythm. "Hofman! Knock it off! Back to the wards, both of ya!" In his heightened awareness, he thought he could actually hear a Marlboro Hard-Pack changing hands.

But the thing was, he needed time to *think*. He did some of his best thinking down below the Stack, below the Main Building, in the tunnels between. And he had a *lot* to think about. All his binary decisions, his dilemmas, were playfully spinning him around on their horns. Burns would be wanting to see him soon, about one thing (his staying, or else being treated like summer help and booted out) while the overreaching PHW had a number of *other* things to discuss. Barnes, in turn, had sent his secretary to meet Rhodes outside his classroom with a note suggesting a meeting time. The gray and large-boned woman had felt it beneath her to perform this service, and the chill had lasted in Rhodes all the way through lunch, when he opened the foul missive:

> *Mr. Rhodes:*
>
> *If you come before your first class, next Tuesday, it will be quite convenient for me. Thus, 9:30.*
>
> *I can't see you after lunch because you have to get to your evening's dissipation. And, of course, this is what we have to discuss.*
>
> *Can't have you being late for Dr. Warthog.*
> *—Barnes*

The overt childishness of this was only one of the chilling things. Oh, *why* was the world so chock-a-block with complete maniacs? Were there *more* or *fewer* outside the loony bin? Why was the tunnel the *only* place of peace within miles? Why couldn't he just *go along*, on the ward, the way everyone else did, instead of staring endlessly at the ripples of such deep water as Anson Fowler?

And when he realized that what really paralyzed him, what had lately made him snappish and almost indifferent to all his other strivings, was Sherrill, he stopped dead. This was the other advantage of the tunnels. You could rant (quietly), you could clutch your skull in bewilderment, you could slap the side of your head and go, "Now see! See, there's another example…" and you could also stop dead without creating a scene.

Thoughts, nearly shapeless, swarmed like bats in the dim reaches. A picture of Sherrill's dad, a boor who worked for a car dealership in a hick area where "dealership," as a term, was a bit grandiose. A disaffected childhood, illicit cigarettes behind the middle school, her door-slamming snarl—violet eyes going blacker, unbearably cute, no doubt—at her parents. Dark struggles in the backseats of cars all through high school. From here Rhodes jumped to a suburban version—his. And a sense of separation. It wasn't the difference between his lush, suburban scene and hers, or anything transcendent in his pawings of innumerable girls in the back of a fairly repellent '70s car. It wasn't even some division that inheres in boy-girl relations. He thought about it for a second. It was the wall created by ten years—that this vision of her was practically yesterday's reality, while his own mirror of it was ten years back. Was this part of her attractiveness? The whole thing could certainly sweep over him, like now, with a sweet ache. A nostalgia that people Sherrill's age didn't feel. Was this a divide between them? Did it separate them impossibly?

Sherrill: a solution to some issues, obviously, connected to ward work and making progress there. But what had been bothering him was more personal. Sure, *sure*, she has to fill in for the other nurses' vacations, hardly makes it to B Ward. Sure, she'd offered encouragement about the *work*. But there hadn't been a word, encouraging or otherwise, about the…about his…

Well, about his need to get her in a certain light to make sure that her eyes were really violet, his need to see the light bounce off her hair when she tipped her beer back, (along with this, an epistemological stumper, *why* was it so charming when she sometimes slurped beer out of the can, forgetting she had a glass?), his need to hear that rare cackle of hers, a sudden teenage dig at the world, his need to find out what she really thought about the old booby hatch (beyond what he saw as her politic ways), his need to find out what she thought about settling down to a career, about all kinds of things, his need to remember what he thought about when he was twenty-one, and, then, you know, the need to know what she thought about…him. Not a word since that night at The Alibi. Not a hint of a warm, not-intimate-but-acceptable, buddy-buddy kind of tone. Silence.

And in the silence of the tunnels, this is where his mind wavered. As summer showed up, above ground, and made all the wan northerners complacent and brown. As the trees went from pale green to dark, and the hay went from green to gold. This is where he began to lose it…

Chapter 33

"The nightmares are of particular interest. Oh, in themselves, of course. But also because they are like the staff of life, the daily bread, of the serfs and psygoads. They are as much the daily fare as the *humble humus* itself. And this is part of the plan. Your body, after all, does get some rest, so that the harvest of justice may continue the next day. And the next, and the next...But the mind, the mind must writhe in torment all through the night, and every night...Ah, the sand of retribution runs through the glass exceeding slow.

"There's the falling. Like the common dream one has of falling, only it doesn't feel like falling off a roof, or out of a tree, a sudden loss of grip. This is more a cold certainty of death, an instant knowledge, yet it keeps on. You fall and fall, you struggle to wake up, you grasp at something to the side of you, it is like the loam, it mocks you with its foamy lack of substance, you get no purchase on it. If your shrieks wake you in the sleep pod, well, they quickly put you back to sleep.

"There's a kind of similar one, with its sickening glimpse of the infinite. Your work furrow lengthens even beyond the horizon. It's as if you are pulled forward, your mind is pulled forward into a nauseating knowledge of some kind, beyond what you actually see, of a furrow measured in time, not space. A related nightmare is the widening furrow. This little darling visits you when your back is aching more than usual. You dream that you turn your burning torso to the side, to heave up a wet double handful of the *humble humus*, and suddenly the furrow widens, so the load falls short, back into the furrow. To the accompaniment of sharp digs from the goad. The delightful sequence is repeated endlessly.

"There's the one where instead of one psygoad driving you on, you have three or four. They contend with each other to stay on top—as it were—of their work, all digging at your back. Their exhortations and critiques combine as gibberish. You strain to understand, to obey, but it is as word salad.

"A related torment is a dream voice, a controller's voice, booming over the fields like that of an old prophet. It originates from a glass pavilion in the center of the controllers' hillside palace, a pavilion six stories high, fully as tall as the Stack. Thus it is an oracular and fearful voice. I've suggested there's no hierarchy among these languid observers. But the one, Anton Farmer, does occasionally act as spokesman. And decidedly you need to be spoken to, after your day of fruitless toil, after your life of…your many iniquities…your foulness. His voice recounts the ways in which you have fallen short, your *inappropriateness* on many levels, your *acting out*. His voice causes great anxiety in your slumbering psyche, almost a physical discomfort. A throbbing arises which feels like an insatiable need to atone.

"These are just samples. You get the picture. In the morning you are led, shattered, shuffling in your shackles, into the fantastic heat of the fields, where the equally drained and hollow-eyed psygoads await you.

"I'm going to move my bowels early today. Goodbye. I… do appreciate your attention. You can in fact be of help."

Chapter 34

Headmaster Barnes, the following week, was, to put it mildly, food for thought. Food along the recurring lines of a chili banquet washed down with ginger brandy and followed by tequila drinking-games at a cheap roadhouse.

Needlessly early, Rhodes thought he would check out the faculty lounge. There he saw only a man who had been pointed out as the hockey coach. Pointed out in tones that suggested a hierarchy such as: Board, Headmaster, Director of Studies, Hockey Coach, lower-case faculty. This man had both hands fiercely propped against the copying machine, which was spitting out math quizzes. A muscular, beetle-browed man. "God!" the man shouted. "I love the smell of hot toner in the morning! It's the smell of...*victory!*"

Waiting outside the H.M.'s office for the ten minutes that Barnes was pointlessly late, and deducting five for transit to the class building, left fifteen for what had been billed as a portentous confab. The large-boned secretary, looking over her glasses at Rhodes in a way that brought to mind the granite-jawed nurses that signed him in at the hospital, stretched the ten minutes uncomfortably.

Finally seated in front of the fat despot, he picked up the expected scent of baby powder and cold cuts, but this time with a nuance of something sour—like the startling B.O. of a woman who'd once picked him up in his hitch-hike in France. Barnes issued no greeting. A clump of gray hair, atop the great knockwurst head, was parted in the middle and looked like a tiny wig. He held a ruler, a thin freebie from the folks at Dead River Gas, and twanged its other end against the desktop. Over and over.

"Rhodes," he sighed, "this will be the latest I've ever written a contract. That is, if you're wise enough to accept our gener—to join our merry little…to hop on our happy little…to be part of this faculty. Which could use someone like you, who doesn't have three heads and whom the kids like. Like enough."

Rhodes became quite sure the ruler was smeared with something like…mayonnaise…and he had no reply. Barnes tossed it aside and pressed on. "What do you know about dyslexia? Hm?"

"Er…nothing, I'd have to say."

"Nothing. Well, I, *I*, as the captain of this…this…anyway, I have made a little study of it. Since—I won't hide the fact—a good many of our students have it, or something similar. In the learning area. And what," leaning forward and inappropriately, it seemed to Rhodes, aiming both forefingers at him like pistols, "what do you think I found?"

"Well, I couldn't tell you."

"No. Pity. Pity you couldn't tell me. But it's this: while verbal processing and language study is a problem for them, Latin, you hear me, Mr. Odes, heh, *Latin* is good for them. Kind of works for them. Something about the…the…Anyway, *we* are going to be forward-thinking geniuses and expand the Latin program here. So, you'd probably have two beginner sections, then one advanced class for your current crew, or intermediate, Cicero or whatever the f—whatever you do with them. Then I need something else for you to do besides watch reruns of *Friends* in the dorm. So we take the Spanish section that jackass LaLumière has, and that becomes yours. As does the Spanish tongue, after some boning up."

"Spanish?"

"Yeah, it's a language. And you're a linguist. And it's a solution. And you can't do any worse than Hippolyte does with it. So. We have the full package. A career, as you might say, on a platter."

Thinking that this was just a tad reminiscent of a Pu Pu Platter, Rhodes picked out one of the items, the yucky Crab Rangoon one. "You mentioned the dorm?"

"Right. Where the kids sleep."

"Er…"

"Part of the package. You realized that, right? A package that pays, in the cash portion, beyond all the other elements…"

The figure was so low that Rhodes's ears began buzzing. He thought he might be flushing red in the embarrassment that Barnes, by rights, should be feeling. He wasn't sure he'd heard right.

"That, plus the dorm, Rhodes, and the meals. And health insurance."

"So, on the *dorm* aspect of it…"

"Yeah, I know. Hard to visualize, if you've never done it. But, in the end, that's what makes this place. It's not a day school. They don't go back to their parents every night. Which makes for, heh, a certain freedom in our dealings with them. *You* become the parent. It ends up being one of the most satisfying parts of the job. You get to watch the little assholes grow."

Long silence.

"Well, OK, good to have all that. Coaching, too, I assume? Happy to coach track, or cross-country. I'll have to th—"

"If you'd be *happy* to coach you'd be very special around here. Too many eggheads already, I have, too much diffidence on the old fields of physical contest. Come on, say yes." He pushed forward a sheaf of papers.

"No, I mean, I'll just need—"

"GODDAMMIT MAN!"

"Wait, I just—"

"You're going to pick and choose and sift the fine points like you're God's gift to secondary education? You're *that* special? I don't have to be a genius with our Latin program, you know, I can just go back to the way it has been and you don't have a job here. You don't have your fancy-pants interminable and delicious *choice* between the goddamn nuthouse and here! You can just rot down there with the whole sad crew."

The man was putting so much feeling into these objurgations that Rhodes, giving it the most creditable interpretation, thought Barnes must actually have the soul of a teacher and care greatly about his school. He didn't know how, or when, to end this involuntary unveiling.

"And get, what," Barnes went on, "a promotion, exactly one, in your whole life? To what, Aide II or something? Psycho Suppressor II? Mud Wrestler II? The best you can do in thirty years down there, with my abhorrent brother, is be in charge of a ward someday?"

"Well, when you put it that way…"

"Did you know my senescent half-brother once deflated my bike tires, when I was fifteen, when I had a sweet date, across town—and hid the pump?"

How would Rhodes have known this?

He started to rise from his chair. Sanity started, once again, to seem like a relative thing when he put this office up against the mental hospital.

"Did you know he goes to *cock fights*?"

"Hah! Well, you make your argument very effectively. I *do* need to think all this over. I'm sure you understand. Just a little time…"

"Yeah you think it over! You get back to me pronto. I have to organize a *semester*, are you following me? *Now*. Goddammit, have you ever seen the man eat spaghetti?!"

Rhodes, looking back on it, was never sure how he left the inner office. The way his psyche remembered it, it was on tiptoes. On tiptoes past the smirk of triumph on the large-boned secretary. Then a gradual lengthening of stride and an organizing tug at the necktie as he approached the classroom building.

The main thing was, per the usual drill in the recent life of Rhodes, he had just spent a chunk of time being shouted at by a complete loon and absolutely nothing had been made any clearer.

Chapter 35

Hoo, boy. Let's just take a break here. So now our young hero has an outline of one career, with not only the outline, but the career itself shaped by an utter maniac. And he has a compressed timeline to follow. And, to be honest, the academy has its attractions. His teaching, after the hellish interview, had been so much fun that he could almost…he could perhaps…he was leaning…Even the Ball-Buster Back Row Boys in Latin class had been fun.

But then, who needed him more? These supremely carefree kids or the ravers on the ward?

Chroniclers are, as Dickens says, privileged to enter where they list. But that is no good to us here. The tale is told as Rhodes saw it in what, for some reason, is called "real time." For other reasons, too, the things that were unclear are to remain unclear. What mysteries lurk in the dark hearts of Burns and Barnes? What motives might they really have for attaching Rhodes, and others, to their missions? What future attends each choice? How much does anyone (this must include superficial students but surely patients too) really care? Plus this "anyone" takes, more and more, the shape of Nurse Langdon. How much of this could he just come out and ask her—since some of it is his earnest mental hospital stuff (and how earnest is she, anyway, about the same stuff?), and the rest of it is, well, not the kind of stuff you can just blurt out. Yet. If he said, "No, but, what I'm trying to say is how great working with you is. Working alongside you, getting to know you. Because I think you're…you're special, I think you're great. I'm attracted to you," the risk is huge, the risk is tremendous, that her violet eyes would widen. Widen in silence.

Well, do you think our man is hollow inside? Do you think him made of pillow-stuffings? Is he as the willow branch in the wind? None of it! And so he called her, or, er, not having had the courage to get her number, he left her a note. In Minnie's office, since, as he said, "She hasn't been on the ward and I need to get in touch about our project. You know. Our thing we're working on."

And his halting, awkward thoughts had taken this form:

Sherrill—

I desperately need your attention. To our project. I'm getting nowhere with the crew, and there's no point involving the replacement nurses. Maybe there's a work-around we can come up with, so the two of us get it laid out, then ram it into place after we get it all approved? We need to strategize. I think this would require more beers than last time. I'm quite sure dinner would be required. To do a good job.

You seem to have some Fridays off—I have two a month. I know you can master the schedule—that's why you're getting the big bucks. Hah!

Your thoughts?

It transpired that they were seated together in the green and gilt luxury of Restaurant Srinagar just ten days later.

But the ten days, without bringing much else to relate, did bring two dim creatures along to circle Rhodes in the dark lagoon of his doubts. One was Barnes, that is, a new Barnes, the one who had Rhodes's phone number. No doubt equipping himself with this at the desk of the large-boned secretary, Barnes now felt free to make the lapse of ten days seem like a cataclysm, and to call at the oddest hours. He had called once, very late, sounding kind of gurgly and indistinct.

"Rhodes, you have no idea…of the—Listen to me! You must call me in the morning. I must talk to you. I came within an inch of firing that Hippolyte LaLumière. The scene was atrocious. They tell me I had to be restrained, I have no recoll—You must hear what I'm saying. The place is full of hapless fools. We simply have to…Including the jackals on the Board, who have been after me about standards, about the credentials of the—GET BACK TO ME! Dammit."

This had been played by the inexperienced young prospect in the age-old tradition—much like JFK with one of Krushchev's more intemperate Missile Crisis notes—by ignoring it. By calculating that there was some chance, some evidence even, that Barnes wouldn't remember the call. But, of course, there was no telling when another missile of this type might come screaming toward him, and he was clearly *running out of time.*

The other dim and bad thing occurred to him during a long fit of grooming, and some desperate re-grooming, just before the Srinagar dinner. While it was fine to get Sherrill's help on his professional plan, the patients' welfare and all, because that could lead to his staying at the hospital and feeling of worth there, it was not exactly alright that he was trying to get her involved in another way, that he found her incredibly hot. Pretending (to her) that this part of it was low-key, compared to the patients and all, was OK, because that's what you did. At least at first. But soon, not OK. Because she didn't know he might suddenly dump the whole thing, be in a school dorm and some sweaty newbie-orientation by the end of August.

He'd still been thinking over this last bit of discomfort as he headed up the steps into the restaurant. She was there, at a table, and new and minor embarrassments came along to help clear his mind. The place was empty. Rhodes laughingly approved whenever this happened, but realized it made other people feel they'd blundered. After working on some beers, they were handed menus by the most friendly-while-not-at-all-helpful waiter South Asia had ever produced. When he came back with a second beer for Sherrill, they asked about the many unintelligible choices. *The pied yumplings. The blazed beast. The ferries in chocolate.* They goofily settled on a few, since each, it seemed, was a "veddy nice Kashmiddy deesh." Well then.

"Let's saddle up, pardner," she invited, gesturing toward his Bass Ale, his first. "I thought you were serious."

Mistaking the meaning of "serious" for a split second, Rhodes retorted, "No, go ahead. Enjoy your second, perhaps third, tiny canister of pee-colored water while I work on this imperial pint of thick British stuff. Don't worry about me."

She snickered in a way he'd seen before but had forgotten, eyes sidelong, as if sharing with people at another table, her smile a little lopsided. Creating for Rhodes an image of her as the sharpest wisecracker in her tenth grade history class. Not the college-bound section. The other one. He reeled, damn near in love, feeling that the vocabulary of his evening was escaping him. Something about…wasn't there something about…yes, hospital stuff, the ward…a plan. He decided to give it time, give himself time to calm down. Just then he was jolted by the thought—mixed with a feeling he couldn't identify—that she might never get down to planning, to really caring about the nagging frustrations of the ward.

Darned interesting wall-hangings helped him over the moments when he couldn't think of anything to say. And she got going on nursing school, also on her high school, Penobscott, that he'd driven by a few times. Pretty hick, and her wild years had a boondocks flavor, the expected details about booze and cars, sneaking out on a pair of pretty sad parents. No mention of boys.

The food provoked mirth. It looked alive, because it was glistening and so clearly organic while taking on never-imagined shapes and colors. The place remained empty, and Rhodes craned his neck to see into a little bar area—research for the future. It was empty too, except for staff who were peering back.

On her fifth beer and no bathroom breaks—Rhodes was worshipful at this point, his third Bass—she suddenly cut in with, "You know, starting with Elwin, Moose, on this thing, might seem simplest, but I'm not sure it's the way to go."

"Elucidate."

"What?"

"Go on."

"Hey, I know what elucidate means, OK? Why the fuck are you talking like that?"

"Sorry. Look, here's the thing. When you talk, when you're serious and I'm looking at you, I get—"

"Harry. *Harrison*, heh. Here's what you need to get." She frowned and moved her beer aside, as if intending to use the table to sketch out plans. "If we say we want to work more with Morrill, and part of that is getting more input, real psych input from others, you know, Burns and all, they'll say skip it, he's B.O.S."

"Right, but that's when we say, 'Well what does that *mean* to anyone—we need help with understanding that, as a program going forward, especially—'"

"No, because that's when *they* say, like a Catch-22, 'He was burned out twenty, thirty years ago. There's no notes from back then, no family, and the psychosis is burned out. He's completely out of touch with reality, but there's no psychotic ideation going on. There's nothing to talk about.'"

"Ugh. Shit, you may be right."

"Or to talk about with *him*."

"So…"

"So, and I know you brought this up already, someone like Anson Fowler has some history, at least a family—there's some kind of problem there, but maybe there's someone we can talk to—and you can talk to *him*…And his friggin' find munctions. Uh, mind f—"

"Wow. You got something there. So we start with him after all?"

"Such were my thoughts, Tonto. You're catching on quickly."

Rhodes slumping back, as charmed with her mockery as with her spoonerism.

"And I gotta go," she added, grabbing her purse. "Thanks," leaving with startling speed.

Fighting the need to drain an ocean of British export out of himself, Rhodes impatiently paid up and chased after her. A surge of joy, seeing her right near the Srinagar, where she'd parked. As she fumbled in her purse, he put both hands on her upper arms and dove in for a kiss. She looked up, kissed him very quickly on the lips and, even more quickly, found her keys, and was gone.

Chapter 36

"And what body are *you* in? Ever so many ever so many! I'm following my lead. Following my lead. Wallowing in my feed. I simply can't *imagine*. Why is everyone staring at themselves? It's *glandular*. So many secrets. We'll not see his likes again! Such a glandular old fellow. I'm trembling fall over. Catch me if you can! No enema for me, thanks eversomuch eversomuch."

This from the Wild Man, on a bathroom trip. Rhodes had to stay with the quietly padding nudist, with his affable conversation, his good eye-contact. And he had to get him locked up again. But he didn't give it his best; he could hear Fowler warming up in the smoking area.

"You reptiles! You intellectual pygmies! This latest outrage—this burst of foulness—will not go unmarked. You whores!"

Rhodes joined him as soon as he could, trying to clear his mind of the almost nauseating dissonance the two men had set up. He found Fowler more tense than usual, both hands hooked into the window screen, shouting as if there were no glass and a convention of psychoanalysts had assembled in the courtyard below.

He seemed aware of Rhodes, and cranked up the volume. "You wouldn't know a useful bit of therapy from the most hellish act of cruelty. You wouldn't know psychotherapy if it jumped up and buggered you with your own naive textbooks! You filthy swine. You filthy, squirming, suppurating, aimless little hop-toads. You annelids.

You sack of chattering cockroaches. I'll bring the whole thing down on you, I'll bury you under the entire load of your decades of malpractice, the truckloads of excrement your minds have produced. Your boatloads of benighted and hyposensitive pseudoscience. You scurrying pea-brained little rodents, you silverfish in the library of real science. You maggots!"

Rhodes was less certain of his role than usual. Something must have happened. How to help? "I'm listening, Anson. Here for you, man."

"These turds at the picnic of humanism! These pretenders in the temple of science. They are the termites in the foundation of this building, a *hospital*, a place that, in theory, does have some usefulness. Their glistening avid little mandibles, their fat white abdomens—it's too much for me! The horror of it, the horror of their society, of having to talk to them, ask them favors. These puling, conventional, jargon-fed intellectual babies. What comes out of their mouths is indistinguishable from the shit they sit in all day! I can't take it, I just...I..."

Rhodes was still searching for a response when Fowler turned part way toward him, before walking away, and explained, "Once again I'm denied a visitor."

Chapter 37

"No, bring your hands where I can see them!" The hapless goad has been made to sit on a high steel affair, a bit like a barber's chair, in a dank recess of the hillside palace. This way the controller has an easy glance at his bare feet. He bends to look at the soles. "Wiggle your toes. Hm. Right. Well we won't beat about the bush will we?"

The goad stares helplessly at his hands, curling them slightly before a rough woman straps them to the chair.

"And what shade of purple would you call that?" gesturing to the feet, a garish red. "Hm?"

"I—"

"Tut! Don't answer! This is the Talking Cure." (Here a groan from the goad, who has been hoping for a reprieve.) "And who do you think is going to do the talking?"

"Well—"

"Hush! You know the format, I believe. Who, in fact, has the ideas here? The right ideas? Who is it who controls, hm? Who has designed the retribution, the many instruments of justice, the great plan? And just because, in the Great Inversion, you have a title, the oh-so-exalted title of Psygoad, don't think you have anything to say. ANYTHING!" he suddenly shrieks. This controller, with the collection of tics, mood swings and poor grooming of a former mental patient, is just getting warmed up.

The goad, in green Dickie trousers and one of the two hospital-issue shirts (the gray one), gives a sort of whimper.

"What!? You call that talking? Speak up, man!"

"I—"

"SHUT UP! Damn you. Who does the talking here? I do! You don't talk, you listen. Is that so complicated? Honestly, where do we get these useless psygoads from?"

"We—"

"SILENCE! Confound you! Are you deaf? *I* talk. Do we call this the listening cure? No. We don't. That means I don't listen. I talk. And you benefit from my talking." Here a long, casual look at his own fingernails, the artful languor of the professional torturer. "Now, where were we before you so rudely interrupted the…talking. Ah yes, the condition of your feet. Now, what we look for, as you well know, is a particular deep shade of purple. The air-cured humus. A hue we call the color of retribution. It is particularly rich, enjoyable to behold of an evening, as you all return to the cavern to, heh, sleep. And what have we here," gesturing with some disgust toward the feet, "is this purple? Do I detect the slightest shading toward the blue, the mauves, the purples?"

"But—"

"SHUT UP YOU SWINE! GODDAMN YOU! You vile thing! Why must I exhaust myself with talking, trying to cure you. You won't listen. *I* am the one with the concepts. *I* understand the system. *I* have structured it all for success or failure under the rules. In the current…arrangement. DAMN YOU!" He sits back in his easy chair, adjusts his shirt collar and takes a few deep breaths. "Ach…where was I, amidst your constant yammering and baying nonsense. Your screeching need for attention. *I* am talking, goddamn it. Oh yes, the color. Now. Do we see what we'd like to see here, so that the humble psygoad can return to his sleep pod, rather than undergo the usual eighteen hours of the Talking Cure," (yes, the goad has heard about the duration, has hoped it was just a rumor, has disbelieved the stories about what happens to the subject's mind in the final hours, how preferable are the nightmares of the sleep pod), "do we see even the slight purple of a baboon's pink rear end? No, for shame," peering with mock concern, "we don't. Does wishful thinking allow a glimpse, the merest streak, of the purple that steals into a pink sunset? Sadly, no. Could there be a mistake, like a child changing her mind with her Crayola set and rubbing the blue crayon over her red drawing? Hm? So that we see a little, a *leetle leetle beet*, hm? of what WE NEED TO SEE!? No! You shiftless monkey! You dolt!"

"But—!"

"SILENCE! You piece of shit! What is the MATTER WITH YOU!?" The controller once again makes a little show of trying to regain his composure. This kind of thing, a brand of theatrics that offends as well as bores with its cheapness, will go on for many hours. The heart of the psygoad sinks.

The controller crosses his legs and launches into a series of set-pieces, bits he always uses, much in the manner of a filibuster, to draw out the hours. "Perhaps you need to have refreshed for you the vast purpose of the whole affair. The elements of design involved. Yes, it seems clear you don't get it." He arranges his thoughts, clearing his throat and looking at the high vault of the ceiling. "You see, it is *retribution* for your faults in that former...occupation. For all the laziness, your coddling of your own acedia, the times you wouldn't get off your too-casually clad butt if someone spilled something, if someone called out to you, if someone was in pain. Oh, if it were just laziness! Your indifference, your selfishness, your complete lack of care for anything that went on—the general happiness of the population, the ethics of work, the progress of individuals. Also your bovine complacency. The arrant puffery that led you to believe you deserved that salary, or that, in any way, you knew best. For these and many other sins—but particularly for your physical laziness—we have devised what I'm sure you agree we all crave: justice."

"Mecch…"

"SILENCE! You hound! My God can't you hold your tongue! I have so much more talking to do. And you have so richly deserved it. I haven't even gotten to your particular role."

Another little show of collecting his thoughts.

"So. This is why you are on your feet for the fourteen hours. And not only that, but you are moving forward, making, heh, progress in the painfully awkward way enforced by your having to walk in the humus outside the furrow. Surely these details I don't have to explain to you. But the design, the reason for the physical pain that is such a rich part of the fields of justice, perhaps I have now made this more clear. More…reasonable. Now, now that we both understand each other…you must know how offensive is this red on your feet, that you have the nerve to come traipsing in here with…I can barely stand to look at it. However, justice must be done," the controller winds up, briskly.

There follow chunks of doctrinal boilerplate very similar to the forgoing. All tediously introduced with a condescending didacticism. Bits such as: "So. What we have here is evidence that, once again, *to make things easier on yourself,* you have stepped down and walked willy-nilly, sashaying, I suppose, with a wanton disregard for all the norms, in the substrate of the furrow. Instead of in the *humble humus,* the purple product of all our labor. And damaging the furrow, damaging the furrow into which we must plough back the humus tomorrow. Tut tut. Very grave. The most serious type of infraction."

This kind of thing. For another seventeen hours.

All very apt. And, as we say in the retribution business, so richly deserved.

It was after a lengthy exposé of this type that Rhodes, squeezing his skull, stumbled back to the nurses' station and grabbed Fowler's chart. He riffled frantically through it, found what he thought he'd once seen, something about "manic episodes," then, as he remembered, almost nothing in the pages normally devoted to treatment plan, prognosis, and medication. And then he found a few pages, a bit out of place, on history. It seemed Fowler had been born in Louisiana, to sharecroppers. They had moved north when he was five, about twenty years before some "incidents," during his graduate school years, brought Fowler to the hospital.

Rhodes found that, in a way, this didn't help at all. Yet, missing information seemed to cry out some message. He noticed, suddenly, that the history page ended in the middle of a sentence at the bottom, right above a standard footer. The next page had the usual footer, but was blank.

There was no way of telling what was missing.

Chapter 38

The next fiendish visitation to whipsaw Rhodes's psyche like a tattered windsock in a hurricane was a session with Dr. Burns.

He had been summoned to come in a half hour before his shift. He sat in the lugubrious shadow of the office, while Burns, in a gesture curiously reminiscent of…something…held a long pencil by one end and tapped, tap-tap-tap, on the desk with the other end. This went on for some time. Rhodes almost blurted out ill-formed thoughts about B Ward when he stopped himself, remembering that he hadn't initiated the meeting, and that he needed more time with Sherrill before taking the bull by the horns.

"High summer."

"What?" Rhodes stammered, finding the "high noon" tone of this ominous.

"High summer, Mr…Harry. Tall clouds. The hay harvest going apace. The goldenrod and dragonflies about to sally into the picture." Rhodes shot a nervous glance at the florid British poetry next to his chair. "And," a heaving, creaking attempt to bring himself closer to the desk, partial success in bringing his bulging features into better light, "the time of year when I think about shit-canning some of the summer help. And good *guh*…oo-widdance to some of those Mongoloids."

"Aren't they called Down—"

"They're called whatever the Unit Director calls them, OK? So, in this case, if you follow, Mongoloids. And listen to me, we don't need any hoity-toity *guh*...oo-wevisionism around here, that's not what I'm looking for."

"What..."

"SO! So, since I was trying to develop a thought along these lines: what I'm looking for in *you*. As opposed to those unwashed who will be leaving campus in a few weeks. You who, one is disposed to think, will be *staying*." Burns cast an almost spiritual gaze at the ceiling, mulling not so much word choices as values, the values of a Burns Ward. "I want your education, your c.v. anyway, sans the nouveau vocabulary that might come with it, the weenie fancy-ass jargon and some of the notions that are part and parcel. *And* I've made this clear to you. *And* it's high time you showed some f—, some damned decisiveness."

"Well I—"

"AND ANOTHER THING. While it's not clear to me what murky attractions you may find in the creepy prep school up north, I do think you're unaware of what a howling lunatic you'd be working for."

Rhodes's mouth sagged open. He snuck a glance at his watch. The pencil tapping began again.

Burns went on, with a little more vigor. "Do you know he once had the buildings and grounds people lock everyone up in their dorms—students and faculty—and fed them nothing but crackers for two days, while he harangued the campus with a bullhorn? About what? About litter, soda cans, and so on."

"Well, now that you mention it, he is a bit—"

"He goes through about two secretaries a year. The faculty are fleeing in droves, they clog the highway."

"Hah! Well, to be perfectly—"

"The strangest noises come out of his living quarters. Exciting the interest of the *guh*...oo-wustic constable in the village..."

Rhodes, rising, "Well, I'm off to the ward. I do underst—"

"You're off to the ward BECAUSE I SAY SO! Damn it, man. You have another week. I can… I can come up with some incentives. You make an appointment. You get back to me!"

A total rout. Well, no, not really, because it wasn't a *total* rout until this was added:

"I'm making some changes. You can shelve the warm and fuzzy shit for a while. I'm bringing in Mavis LaCroix as Supervising Nurse."

Chapter 39

Why, oh why was it so difficult to ask Sherrill for her phone number? Well, it was somewhat fun, passing notes. And this kept things professional. But both lines of attack on the sanctity of her thoughts required more time. More tête-à-tête. Especially with the new and explosive Burns countdown.

But it *was* difficult. She steered him off somehow. Now why was that? There was a moment when Rhodes thought that maybe, just maybe, she didn't…like…men. This problem had arisen at several key junctures in his life. Putting it delicately to one side for the time being, there was the question of a more general evasiveness. The aura, the force field, the kryptonite wave coming off her. And that, in his tiny, hot, barely-furnished apartment, needed four frosty beers and a good evening of thought.

In one great, crystalline moment—the same instant in which the glow of his open refrigerator revealed three remaining beers—he realized she might be trying to transfer off B Ward. Nothing negative to do with him, really, but causing her to hold back from the relationship. This relatively painless solution was only marred by the thought that, if she left, no one would be helping him with his plans for upgrading the PHWs' function.

Was it the plans themselves?

Was all this too bold for a new nurse?

Well, it wasn't too bold for *him*, and nurses were in demand. She was virtually unfireable unless she really stepped in it. Burns, to be sure, always being a bit of a wild card. And she'd stood up to Van, had had a private talk with Minnie Jewel, and enjoyed her support of the plan.

There was the bold moment, some time after the fourth beer, when it occurred to Rhodes that the hospital might have required her to have a landline. He might be able to find her number, old school, through 4-1-1. In the few seconds before this was cruelly blown out of the sky, he ginned up a couple of warm, pseudo-spontaneous greetings: a Plan A phrase about the patients and the project, along with a Plan B phrase about feeling close to her—without in any way deciding which of these he was going to blurt out.

He subsided into fairly morose imaginings. She'd had a traumatic childhood, was damaged goods. She was, like most people new on the job, open to anything and only hung with him out of sincere interest in his ideas about the ward. She had originally kind of liked him, but had gradually become repulsed, horrified, by his strange enthusiasms, nervous chatter, overly long hair. Perhaps she'd seen his old and startlingly foreign car and decided he was poor (OK, bull's eye there), moreover chronically poor. Maybe she thought he was old. Like the car.

In a slightly better vein, but only slightly: maybe she wasn't trying to transfer off the ward, but had gotten the heads-up before Rhodes did about Mavis LaCroix splitting time with her. So she was holding back—both from any personal relationships and from any plan about how the ward worked.

As to the ward, Rhodes, sliding to the horizontal on his ratty couch, began to see himself struggling and alienated, in tense huddles with Van and the crew, possibly becoming a complete outcast. And having to accomplish something every day, starting tomorrow, in order to know—within Burns's schedule—if it was worth sticking around.

As to his Supervising Nurse, he thought it was best just to drift…to drift off to sleep fixing one image before him: her sidewise little smirk, her slanted smile that sometimes did—but only partly—include him.

Chapter 40

"So guys," he launched in, avoiding eye contact but choosing the moment wisely—just after all the charts were done, clothes picked up, Night Doors done. "How about we get after this idea—maybe a fun idea—I had, and get something done this week, before I'm off. I'll do ninety percent of it. And we'll look good. But, I mean, it could be really satisfying work—" here a peeling, window-rattling fart from Live-Free Lenny, who happened to be on duty, with his trick of looking someone—in this case Rhodes—right in the eye, but slightly lowering his eyelids, kind of a sleepy look. "Nice, Lenny, glad you're listening. And, of course, it's meant to be a team thing, everyone putting in some ideas, some effort." Slight cough.

"Hey, fuck you, Harry."

"Naw, come on, Donny—and Minnie, you know, she wants it done. So...and it won't be hard."

"What have you been here, Harry, three months?" This from Dick Knight. "Why don't you settle in, like, for a year or something, before you start thinking of ways to fuck up my life. OK?"

"So, if you would just *try* some of these things, it's not going to hurt. It'll make the whole effort more enjoyable, I promise."

"Said the bishop to the actress." Filbert's two cents. Expressionless.

"And I'd *like* to get one patient set up, this week, with more of a—"

"And *I'd* like a blow-job from Marisa Tomei, Rhodesie-Boy. But we both know," Dick said, leaning forward with a look of heartfelt concern, "it just isn't in the cards."

There wasn't any Jimmy Galt, enjoying his days off, to soften the shittiness of any of this. Nothing for it but to plunge ahead. Aware of nothing but the increasingly insincere sound of his enthusiasm. The rationale for starting the project with Anson Fowler. The pressured timetable—less than a week to get something on paper for this one patient—which was due to Burnsian motives no one else could know.

And yet he slowly became aware of Drouin's expression, its change to something both open and hard, as he stared over Rhodes's shoulder. Sherrill. Her elbows resting on the half door. How long had she been there?

"Right, and the timing is good," she chimed in, looking blandly at Rhodes. "A week or so, I think you said. Then we have something concrete, we look like a team, a great team, as Harrison said—"

"*Harrrrison...*" Knight fluted out in a mock light-in-the-loafers voice.

Van, who'd been staring at her, got up and opened the bottom half of the door. It opened inward, but he didn't open it far enough—so that, in effect, he shoved past her onto the ward. He walked off coldly, tossing out, "I'm doing census."

"And we take it to the higher-ups," she went on smoothly. "And they like us, maybe shut down some of the rumors I hear about changing our ward management style—"

"*Harrrrison...*"

"Or they don't like it, and you're off the hook for the whole project."

"Yeah, so, with Fowler, just look at the problem," Rhodes pressed on. "What's missing. In the way we deal with him. What we know about him."

"I heard he was a farmer, down South," Knight threw in.

"I heard he hit someone in Tremblay Building." This from Filbert.

Lenny's eyes widened. If he couldn't fart, pretty much *at* the Supervising Nurse, it seemed he was at a loss...

"And that's about it," Rhodes went on. "Notice how a page or two seem to be missing, on history. Nothing for a treatment plan. Nothing you would, you know, hook your comments to, every shift, in some larger context. Speaking of which—"

"Oh jeez..." (collective)

"There's more to say about what's missing. But I even have an idea, a new way to actually write your comments. For everybody." A glance over his shoulder. She was gone—bad news in not just the obvious way. Now he couldn't walk her to the door and get in an extra word or two.

He cleared his throat, lowered his head into Fowler's chart, and charged. "Maybe I'll just try it myself for a few nights this week. On Fowler. Then I'll show you. But it works like this..."

Rhodes was eventually saved by the end-of-shift jostle, by some kind of fatigue that kept the cruel ripostes to a minimum, and by the thought that Day One of the countdown (Sherrill helping) hadn't gone too badly.

—

Chapter 41

Day Two. Because he'd run into Sherrill in Minnie Jewel's office area, eleven o'clock the night before, Rhodes now had this fabulous 1:00 lunch date on Main Street. He was beaming—she'd accepted (unsmiling) so readily.

While waiting for her, his heart—his mood, let's say, to be more modern about it—went to a darkish spot. That girlfriend in undergraduate days. Blonde, quiet, a bit dysthymic. He had thought he was in love (he was?) the day he learned she was head over heels for one of his favorite writers. Not one of the Latin ones—universally viewed as kooky choices—but Gogol. They'd had such great talks about him, and it seemed that this opened up something endless in the girl, in their relationship. Their future. When she dumped him for a meathead Econ major he learned what it was to have—like now—so many things, so many kinds of happiness, depend on one person.

They sat under a huge green umbrella on the sidewalk, awaiting their falafel orders, both blinking in considerable awe at the bustle of the street and its contrast with the cloistered feel of the hospital up the hill. A couple of pedestrians had a familiar look, and their stiff gait, beset by extrapyramidal symptoms, revealed them to be patients with off-grounds privileges. Rhodes swallowed hard and dealt with the way nothing in Sherrill's manner acknowledged that kiss outside the Srinagar. A kiss, were this a novel, that would be called "stolen." Well, fair enough.

"What is *falafel* anyway?"

Rhodes hesitated. "Well… jeez, I don't know. What the heck is it? You'll like it, guaranteed. Let's just say it's a *substance*. An ineffable substance. And we're not to know. And we're happy!"

When it came, Sherrill ate with amazing gusto, making Rhodes smile. She snorted a few times at things he said. All seemed right with the world, but then turned a bit queer.

"Er, Sherrill… I have a couple of thoughts about the ward. Something very concrete to air out. But then, here's the thing. It's something related, concrete, too, about me, about my life. I should… share it."

She looked at him, as earnestly as you might want, still shoveling falafel.

"The thing of it is, if we can't make some of these changes, on the ward, I mean…I just don't see the value in it. Let's say, in what I do there—the point of my being there." He pushed his food away, leaned back.

Someone paused, too close, to stare at them. His dark skin tone—a Thorazine reaction to the sun—and belligerence marked him as *hospital*. "OK, sir, move it along," Rhodes snapped, getting fairly quick compliance. "I mean, the point of my keeping the job."

Nobody, aside from Burns, knew he actually had a toe-hold in another job, and it seemed strange to him now, to be puking up personal stuff without giving Sherrill this key piece.

She, in turn, offered, "Yeah, I see that," with as much appropriate concern as *most* people would want, but *not* the extra dose of *personal* concern Rhodes wanted—the concern for him as a likeable person, someone she would like to keep on seeing. He quickly abandoned the fishing expedition and plunged on with the professional game.

"Well, anyway, hoping for the best. Here's the concrete thing I was building up to. I read somewhere about recording methods, you know, charting and all, and I modified some stuff I read. What about this: every night, every patient gets an observation—not just 'Quiet and cooperative'—that goes under a heading like *Objective*. 'O' for Objective. And you put down a behavior, or something he said, that's a good indication of how he's doing, regressing, progressing, getting wound up, whatever. The beauty there, it forces you to be attentive, and to think a little bit. And you have to have some idea of context— what else is said about him in his chart, diagnosis, plan, also the previous shifts, and so on. Right?"

Sherrill, taking an amazing long gurgle of Coke, kept her eyes on him.

"Then, under 'A,' for *Assessment*, or maybe it's *Analysis*, you put your interpretation of what's going on with him. In relation to what you noted under Objective. *Then*, follow closely here—" Rhodes tried a light note, kind of chuckling at the tightness of his reasoning, as she leaned back and stifled a belch, "under 'P' for *Plan*, you say how all this relates to the really big picture, what the prognosis and treatment plan are. Is. Have—has—always been."

He made a *ta-dah!* kind of gesture, quickly followed by one finger in the air: but wait! "See anything wrong with this picture? By the way, O.A.P., we'll call it…the O.A.P. system, which I'm quite proud of. A little more work for staff, but not a ton more."

"A *little more work* could be more of a problem than you think."

"I know. OK OK, I know. But listen, here's the real problem. You can't get started, you can't install this program, this little gem of a— anyway, and this goes for most of the patients—you can't do it *if there's no explicit treatment plan*." He paused, glaring at her. "It doesn't make sense. There's nothing to hook it into."

She worked with her napkin for much longer than such a cute, and small, mouth could have required, then asked, very calmly, "So, then what? What's the solution?"

"OK, so *then*, what follows from *that*, since I'm not giving up on this, is I go to Burns, I confront him with a concrete example, Fowler. Even without going into the whole plan, unless he's somehow intrigued by it, fat chance is my guess, I tell him 'We can't do any responsible charting, tracking, treatment of any kind with this guy unless we know more about him. History, *recent* diagnostic observations, updated treatment plan.' Just hit him with it. Maybe leave the raw ethics of it unsaid, but just, like, come on man, how are we going to treat this guy responsibly. And he's not the only patient on B Ward. See what he says to that!"

Rhodes slowly let the air out of his balloon, sat back, realized, as he had once before on the ward, that he'd said his piece the way he'd meant to, that it was the best he could do.

But, as he headed toward campus, he also knew it was just the beginning. Heavy lifting ahead. Maybe the beginning of the end, but still a steep beginning.

And Sherrill, as she sped up the hill in her separate car—well, we don't know what she was thinking, do we?

Up on the ward, Rhodes was tasked with getting vital signs from Davey Doucette. As he put the blood pressure cuff on, he asked, "How you doing today, Davey?"

Davey was several days into a low phase in his mania, the mood swing pretty much dragging on the ground. Impossible to imagine his earlier frenzies, his go-go dance on the smoking room table. No answer.

"The last few days have been rough, I know." Davey's face looked ten years older than it did in his hyper-manic phases. He looked more wrinkled, his eyes seemed set differently, with more of a downward slant to the outside. The shocking difference, though, was the look in them. They seemed a darker color, and completely without expression. It seemed possible to sink in them to an infinite depth, but only because they reflected nothing human, nothing of feelings, nothing of motivation.

"Harry," he murmured, in a faint voice, the most distant echo of his usual bubbly greeting. He didn't move a muscle.

"I know it's rough," Rhodes repeated. "The meds, you know, they will even things out. You'll bounce back." He left Davey and for several minutes felt a sadness he'd never felt before. It was a deep empathy for the depressed well he'd looked into, but it was something more. He felt contaminated by a kind of wisdom, as if Davey knew something, knew the sadness fated for all humans.

Soon he was standing with and contemplating a slightly agitated Anson Fowler, who seemed to have been waiting for him, and who launched into a high-pitched extension of his favored scenario. He looked away, to the far playing fields, and started in—but with a newly fierce look, slightly baring his teeth.

A rabid raccoon had once shown Rhodes a very similar face.

The serfs, of course, as opposed to the goads, are also punished. The pathetic, squirming...Oh, how they are punished! Be they Herr Blisters, Dr. Ubu, Professor Simpers, or a groveling hoi polloi of serfs— no matter. In a special twist, they are sometimes punished together, all of them, for the transgressions of the one.

Their "talking cure" is especially is especially is especially... ah, harrowing. At the end of its forty-eight hours they are shrieking, straining at their leather cuffs, begging to process back out to the furrows.

A frequent infringement on the decorum of the Great Inversion, a particular mockery of its logic, is the serf's insulting of the psygoad. Calling him (muttering over his shoulder to one of the serfs behind him in the same furrow) a "psycho." Those caught in this wanton...this flouting...this nearly insane breach receive a punishment of mid-range severity.

All the goads and serfs sleep with their pods tilted back at sixty degrees. For the serfs, the pressure on the many goad-sores of their backs is a discomfort which keeps them, all night long, from the deepest sleep and makes the nightmares more acute. As an awful nightly megrim seeps into the cavern, matronly types, whom I've called wardens, tuck them in by whisking any muck off their feet with a stiff brush, giving the hue of hands and feet a last check, and clipping the pod shut. ("Did we have a good day with the humility humus, dearie? Dig enough of the duty dirt? Hm? The loony loam? Nighty-night, then."—You may judge with what sarcasm, as they clip them in.) Now, the serf who is doing penance for his essentially psychotic lack of respect has the back of his pod slightly heated. The heat is maintained all night. The inflamed sores from a day's goading eventually feel like cigarette burns.

Hoo, boy! The matrons administer enough gas to put the serf to sleep, but the nightmares revolve around the pain, which is still felt. And thus, through many other…so many other…little measures is…*order*…preserved. The new order of things.

Turning with a slightly bored look, at last, towards Rhodes, he handed him a letter.

"I know you'll do the right thing with this." After a pause, which felt like the most human moment they'd shared, Fowler went on, "I'm sorry, it needs a stamp."

It was addressed to an Angeline Fowler.

Rhodes didn't question for a second that he would put it in the mail.

Chapter 42

"C-c-c-cun—!"

"Jim! James! Settle down! Enough o' that!"

It was only a Tuesday, Day Three in Rhodes's scheme, but it still portended what a really "high" ward could look like.

Van had to yell at Jungle Jim over the Dutch-door, while inviting Rhodes to sit down for a heart-to-heart. His compact, sandy-hued face and body seemed a little tense at the desk. Nothing new there. "OK, Harry. We'll see where this goes, this thing of yours. There's nothing anyone can say against it, except it's a little more…work. We do it for a week, good idea to tackle one patient, see how it goes. Even if you and I end up doing most of it, get the chart looking better, run some of it up to Minnie while we're doing it, it's worth getting it done."

Rhodes was breathing a little more freely than he had in weeks.

"*Then*, at that point we let the dust settle a little. Biting off a small chunk makes it easier to sell, for one thing. But also, we have to see if Burns and everyone is really going to buy in. Into something a newcomer plucked out of his ass in this way, Rhodesie."

"Right, it's new, but based on some things—"

"Yeah. I'm sure. You're a smart cookie. But there's more to being smart around here than—" and here this hard-to-read individual clearly struggled for the other half of the comparison, sensing the virtue of everything readable in Rhodes's eyes, his face, his position over the last few weeks, "—than, you know, what's perfectly logical and right for the patients." His expression, despite some effort, revealed how lame this felt to him.

Suddenly they noticed Iggy parked at the Dutch-door. The odor of his skin alerted them. How long had he been there? His tiny eyes burned with intelligent malice.

"Yes, Iggy?" Van asked, not bothering to hide his annoyance.

"Oh," Iggy shoved off, not bothering to hide his mendacity, "just wondering who's on as nurse tonight."

"You'll be the last to know. Just after we do."

When she did appear, she was a vast disappointment to Rhodes, stumbling onto the ward in the form of Mavis LaCroix. She stumbled because she came in from the A Ward stairs, at the spot where Rhodes and Van were wrestling with Roy Houle, an unusually strong mental patient. His visits to B Ward were usually the result of whiskey-fueled assaults on police in the far north, and he was generally respected because he didn't seem that cuckoo, and because of his massive arms and shoulders.

Van gained control of the situation by a technique new—aside from civilian life—to Rhodes: the nut-grab. Gazing at Houle and completely expressionless, he squeezed. Houle's yowls were eventually accompanied by discernible weakness in his limbs. Van squatted over him, squeezing away. "Van Hoek, you fuckin' queeyah! You fuckin' queeyah! You faggit!"

Filbert and Galt came running and, over this din, Mavis calmly issued orders, "I'll get the door, just get the arms and legs for me." She meant the door to the rubber mattress room, the bed with the four-point restraints permanently in place. Dick Knight came running, back from calling his bookie, and, with a little more sweat than usual and two men on the arm that was snapping Filbert back and forth, the deed was done. Much panting, sidelong glances at Mavis.

"Alright, book it and check him every fifteen," she snapped. "I'm going to see what kind of shape the day shift left us in." She moved off in a fast, jagged stomp, bent slightly forward. Mavis was around fifty, her gray hair in the kind of perm that Rhodes associated with a certain north country vintage. No-nonsense glasses over darting blue eyes. She wagged her square jaw sparingly and had never been known to smile.

"Oof!" was Galt's estimation of the situation. "Guess we gotta keep our shit together tonight."

"It's inopportune that the ward seems to be going high," was Filbert's appraisal.

A couple of probing glances toward Van, incomplete endorsement, let's say, of the nut-grab, plus predictable curiosity over how he was handling being called a faggot by such a rugged customer. Then back to the nurses' station for some extra paperwork, the fans turned up to high after this dust-up.

Sure enough, there was a fight over which TV show (in the plexiglass box) to watch, Davey Doucette was put on suicide watch, and Iggy provoked three patients into improprieties, just for fun, so that they lost their smoking time.

At a certain point, during a lull after the march back from dinner, the Wild Man's face appeared in his little window, slathered in blood. Always locked up, naked and pacific, this time he was seen ferociously biting his thumb. He seemed bent on biting it off.

Rhodes and Galt had to pin him against a wall while Filbert and Van dug out a complete set of restraints from the laundry room. They had to rig up another bed, a process that went on for more than fifteen minutes, during which Rhodes tried his best—though two-way conversation had never been a Wild Man thing.

"Come on, come on now, slow down. We don't gnaw on the body parts, OK? Not appropriate." He realized that self-satire wasn't really what was called for. "We'll fix up your thumb, and you're going to lie down for a while. We'll…talk later, OK? Just settle down."

"It's gnosticly appropriate! It's *gnosticly* appropriate! Don't tell me to die down! I'm a phantasm! A hand spasm! Fuck me!"

More paperwork, and a sense, the professional sixth sense in these places, whereby even the laziest and most careless staff gradually become aware that they have to be on their game, that the whole evening is going to be chancy. That the shift notes are going to get extra attention. From the higher-ups.

When Mavis came back to pass meds she went immediately to the Wild Man's restraint room. "Hey!" she barked. They found he'd worked his head over to one side, and was able to bite effectively at his thumb. "How long has this been going on?"

"I noticed it a while ago," Knight started to explain. "I tried tightening the cuffs…"

"Get me a sheet!"

"What…?"

"Get me a sheet—from the laundry room. Get going!"

Rhodes watched in growing awe as Mavis, not allowing herself a smile, commented, "An old Indian trick." She rolled the sheet into a long rope, then wound it very adroitly in a somewhat complicated pattern around the patient's head and neck. "Tie the ends to the bed."

When they had done this, it was suddenly clear that this smallish, hard-bitten woman—rumored to be an alcoholic—was worthy of her legend. Wild Man's head couldn't move more than an inch.

And what followed from that, after still more minor rhubarbs on the ward, more paperwork, was an odd trepidation deep in our young hero. It was connected to an ongoing issue: what was his place in all this? How was he worthy? What long-term dedication, and force, did he have, compared to Mavis? What long institutional history was he unaware of, what deep knowledge did people like Mavis, perhaps Burns, have—that kept a place like this running? Were there hidden strengths of aberrant personality that he should start emulating, or at least respecting—that were able to keep control of a hospital like this?

And were able, year after year, to keep a rumpus room like B Ward under control.

It was a somewhat queasy Psychiatric Health Worker who slunk home at 11:00.

Chapter 43

In his dream, Rhodes is fairly comfortable in a booth at The Alibi. This must mean something in itself. Over Sherrill's shoulder he can see the fat woman punching the arm of her wizened companion. Rhodes is fairly comfortable because Sherrill, although expressionless and stirring a rather fancy grownup cocktail, is listening to him. And he's pouring his heart out.

That is, he's rectifying what has felt to him like a dishonesty. He is very earnestly, over and over, explaining his ambivalence about the hospital. It feels good, it feels as though he's on a date, it even seems that he's connecting with her.

And it feels good because he's getting it out, all the reasons—*job* reasons—why he's ambivalent about staying. And in the pervasive dream reality, it makes sense. Up to a point. The things he says, over and over, make sense—about the job. And he keeps insisting, "It has nothing to do with you." This makes him feel honest. In the pervasive dream logic, she knows about his feelings for her; they can put that part aside, in all forthrightness, in this discussion. This earnest discussion.

But in the morning it's gobbledygook. Because she doesn't know. This fact deriving somewhat from his being an ass. The arguments, the pros and cons that bat him back and forth in the great badminton court of eros and ethos before he drops off to sleep, they, in fact, have to do with her, alongside the hospital.

When is that going to come out?

Chapter 44

On the good side, he now had her phone number. Was this ever going to lead to some clarity? For him? For her?

Day Four on the ward kicked off with Stan Mikita having a seizure. As Rhodes knelt on the green linoleum and gently braced his head, he looked at the racked face and thought about a life punctuated by these skull-storms. A long life, at the hospital for no reason other than that no one wanted him. Never knowing when the next attack was coming, hoping the hockey helmet would protect him when he fell, being dazed for hours afterward.

But Rhodes thought more about the life in between such moments. A parallel suggested itself: his own life on the ward, long hours of boredom shattered by sudden violence. Was he the same after each of these, or lesser in some way? What did his future hold, viewed that way?

Back to Stan—was his quality of life even less than it had been, after each seizure? Rhodes realized he didn't even know the answer to that— he'd been too lazy to read the article he'd seen on long-term epileptics.

The seizure happened in the smoking area, and seemed to irritate Anson Fowler. So there was, it seemed, something off-center—in that it was wildly self-centered—about this man. It was clear the irritation came from not being able to fire up his narrative with Rhodes. He was looking from one person to another—from Rhodes to Stan to others—

as if there was a genuine alarm in his own narrative, a genuine crisis where the grapes of retribution are stored.

It seems that one of the serfs, not content with his lot of humility and simply muttering "psycho," has wrenched his head around in the furrow and spat the word directly at his goad. This, accompanied by some kind of physical threat.

The psygoad bade his time—perhaps out of timidity, for they are a timid herd—and later, currying favor no doubt, told one of the wardens. The serf was clipped into his sleep pod by one of these. She and her colleagues maintained the blandest of expressions throughout. Then a phalanx of them went to the controllers to confer about a punishment.

The cautiousness of these proceedings arises from a rumor: the errant serf is Superintendent Pee-Stains.

The selfless wardens, of course, need their sleep. They are dismissed. This is the hour when the controllers normally unwind (still more), reclining on couches to eat Sicilian cold cuts and slices of mango while reading Eastern poetry to each other. Quite a stir has been caused.

Eventually, Anton Farmer, whose counsel is always valuable, weighs in. He quickly arms himself with a stout goad staff and descends to the cavern. The handful of wardens still on duty escort him down a long line of inclined pods. The problem, the horror show that *loss of control* entails, begins when they find Superintendent Pee-Stains's pod empty.

The controllers' long night of insane chaos kicks off with this observation. In the end, it is learned that Pee-Stains has effected his pod escape in the following manner: For months he has allowed a thumbnail to grow. Every night he folded it under during extremity inspection, and it grew to a length of an inch and a half. On the Night of Insane Chaos, while waiting to be clipped into his pod, he cut and peeled the horrible purple excrescence on the sharp edge of the pod. Then wedged it into the clasp. The plump warden noticed no unusual resistance, clipped him in, but insecurely. When most of the wardens had retired, Pee-Stains popped the latch and emerged like a hellish pupa, to scurry the length of the cavern in search of a hiding place.

"Arm yourselves!" Farmer barks. The controllers, a somewhat effete bunch it must be admitted, in circumstances like these, are not even sure where the goading equipment is kept. "Here they are!" one of them gaily shouts, and they all equip themselves, clumsily, and stand around waiting for orders.

"Fan out!" Farmer yells, and sprints to one end of the cavern. He reasons that there is no way out. His plan is to work systematically back, looking behind every pod. In crisp, soldierly tones he tells the other controllers to start at the far end and work toward him.

It is Farmer himself who finds him. Pee-Stains is clinging to the underside of a pod and has inched around to one side, hoping that as Farmer bends down to inspect he won't see him. But Farmer's rapier-like glance pounces. He makes a grab, but his hand finds only a shirt-tail, slimy with purple goop. And Pee-Stains is off.

The next phase is a Dantesque vision of dark terror that none of the controllers will ever forget. For the true evil of Pee-Stains becomes clear. He runs down the line of glinting, crystalline pods, unclipping as he goes. Serfs and psygoads stagger forth, blinking and bewildered. They soon clump together, mutter their confused, subdued mutterings, and eventually figure out that some great reversal is afoot. They begin chasing down the controllers. They seize extra goad staffs, tear a few more from the hands of the controllers, and begin harrying and beating their superiors, who can find no shelter but the backside of the pods. Knots of serfs can be seen, in the flickering light, tripping controllers with the sticks, then gleefully prodding the fallen bodies. Others back controllers against the cavern wall and, unable to shed the timidity to which they are long inured, make inconclusive, caveman gestures with the staffs.

Farmer, with strategic focus, looks over the writhings and howlings of this confused scene and takes action. Ignoring the more successful posses of serfs, he yells to his cohort, "Find Pee-Stains!" After much time he is found, and the controllers begin to surround him.

Once again, the wily Superintendent deftly turns the tables. He grabs one of the few shrieking, helpless wardens and makes a hostage of her. Backing toward the exit to the fields, he drags her behind him. The controllers pause, hesitant. What does this remind them of? Something from one of their movie marathons in the Pavilion...

"Get him!" Farmer commands. "Hit him with your goads!" But the serf has already ripped a key off the fainting matron's waist and is jamming it into the great door.

As the controllers crowd around the portal their last glimpse is of a galloping, leaping figure, far in the fields of justice. Glimmering, dark mauve furrows in the last rays of the fierce sunset. He is shouting. Something like "You'll lose your privileges! You'll lose your privileges!"

Both hands were once again clutching the thick screen. Fowler's eyes were bugged out, his teeth bared, hair wild—Rhodes had never seen him quite like this. Had something in his ideation brought on this sudden crisis? Or something external—news he'd heard on the ward, or from outside? Something had to be behind it.

Fowler was wheezing, over and over, "You can't tell who's in control!"

So then, at 9:30, the usual peaceful hour, Rhode breaks out his plan. Again.

Van chips in, "OK, guys, we're trying this out. Listen up."

"So, I hope it's agreed, on Fowler, we start with him."

"Why, again?" from Drouin.

"Well, it doesn't matter, but he is calm—uh, most of the time. He can order his thoughts. You could have a conversation with him. We could ask stuff about his past, what he thinks his treatment plan should be, what he thinks he's doing on B Ward. We'd have plenty under the Objective, that heading, in my charting scheme, to quote him on. For example."

"But he's a dick."

"Well, no, Donny. I'm not sure that's the...appropriate handle here. He's just angry at the administration. About some things. Wouldn't you be?"

"Couldn't say. I'm not a fucking mental patient."

"Ok, well, in some ways that's what we're talking about. In what way is he a mental patient? How did he get here, get labeled that way? What terms, and prognosis, should we apply to him, to make that stick? That he is, in fact, mentally ill and needs our help. In specific areas."

Some yawning, stretching, thumb-twiddling and armpit-scratching followed this. Van seemed to preside without actually providing any boost.

Rhodes went on, "This is maybe a side issue, or just a part of the whole thing, but I think the way we write shift notes in the charts is pretty useless. What if we had a system that everyone followed. Like what I was trying to get to the other night. For one thing, quality wouldn't vary too much. The main thing is it would be more informative. I mean, aside from forcing us to pay better attention, to engage—to make observations, maybe even generate more interaction by talking with patients a bit more, in a way that comes from the treatment plan and also contributes information to it."

Phew. Got that out roughly right. To, at least, a kindly nod from Jimmy Galt.

"Anyway, I have this idea, O.A.P.. Every night, you write an O. an A. and a P. for each patient. Standardized, and you have to have something under each one."

"Great," Dick Knight cut in, "and for Moose? I don't care what those stand for, I'm putting nothing under each one. Right? What are

141

you going to say about him? He was nice and quiet, he didn't crush anyone. Come on!"

"OK, but that's my point. When's the last time anyone talked to him? You might get something going. What if you found out some shit, found out what he's thinking?" This was greeted, in the politest version, with more thumb-twiddling and pursed lips. "So, anyway, here's my system. 'O' is for—"

"Osshole." (Drouin.)

"Great. Thanks. 'A' is for—"

"Asinine plan. Not to be implemented." (Filbert.)

"'P' is for—"

"Please tell me you're joking." (Knight.)

"Not joking. And my understanding is we're doing this. Climb on board, guys."

"Give him a break, let's get the details, come on." (Van.)

Rhodes took a deep breath. "So there it is. After you have some interesting times on the ward, instead of just sitting around, you come in here and you have something to say in the charts. It's not tons more work—"

"BULLSHIT!" Drouin was now sitting forward, taking a principled stand, on the labor issue.

"You know what, Donny," Rhodes spat out, slamming Fowler's chart shut, "why don't you go fuck yourself."

Drouin sprang forward, lithe and violent, as Rhodes had seen him do before, but Knight's basketball height was soon between them. "You're an asshole, college boy. Everybody knows it!" And, as he was being diplomatically massaged back toward his chair by the super smooth Knight, "Eat shit!"

Rhodes took a deep breath. "So, since this is such a solid plan, and we're into it, each PHW writes notes of this kind, all three shifts. Except one person, who writes them the old way and looks like a douchebag."

142

"Harrison." This from over his shoulder. At the Dutch-door. Mavis. And how long had *she* been standing there? "Come here. I need you."

"Yeah, but I'm in the middle of—"

"You're in the middle of helping me. Come with me."

Out on the ward, not excessively querulous, he asks her, "Hey, I was doing something important in there. What is this?"

"And now you're doing something important out here. Everything is equally important in the hospital. You'll eventually learn that."

"OK, what is this important thing?"

She shot him a glance, "Laundry room. I need you to count the sheets."

"What!?"

"In you go," she gestured to the door as she unlocked it, revealing not only that there were a great many items to be counted, but that they had just been delivered and not yet put away. "Towels too. And put them all away."

"What the f—"

She took a long, appraising look at him, though, in truth, the appraising had probably taken place before. "Like I say, this is as important as anything else. Why wouldn't it be? This is a *service* to them." She jerked her thumb toward the row of bedrooms, and a probative, nay judicially final, glint came into her blue eyes.

"And the night shift has nothing to do all night, and could be doing this. I mean, if you think anyone is really pilfering sheets. While I—"

"While you continue to make waves. Listen, you don't know what you don't know—about this place. Why don't you hang around long enough to know that, first. And then see if you really want to know what you don't know. Or if you just want to go along."

"The going along could be smoother, is what I think…"

"Nobody cares what you think, just for starters." Did she regret saying this? "Sorry, where was I? Oh yes, *then*, when you know what you're talking about, maybe you can be a little louder. You can figure out what your role in this place will be." She turned toward the door.

"That's what I *am* trying to figure out!"

"No. You're creating a role out of thin air. You're being *creative*. Right now your role is counting sheets, OK? Bring the count to me in Minnie's office after the shift."

Did this wounding encounter help him decide between hospital and school?

Hah! The reader may judge.

But many things, OK, *creative* things, were contributing a certain momentum, and, too, he had been hoping to finally be tight with Nurse Langdon—at a disappointed *minimum*, to be allies with her. So he stowed his parachute once again.

He'd left her a voicemail a couple of days before, and she'd been working A Ward and some wards in the Hemphill Building. So, of course, he was expecting to hear from her. At a *minimum*. A sinking feeling, now, was hard to allay. His fault? Had he blown it once again? But this was the beauty, as he'd rehearsed it so many times, of his situation! He could pour all his earnestness into her ear in the guise of their rebel cause. Right? She could make what she wanted of the tone. His excited, earnest tone. It hadn't, yet, taken him over a cliff.

But, OK, yes, that was a tad chickenshit. What had his voice message said?

"So, looks like you're pulled away from the ward. I really need to talk to you. You've been so great…," (here, flinching again) "and so much help with the project." Here a pause. Way too long. "The thing is," (but he *doesn't say* what the thing is, does he?) "I need a wingperson, you know, on this, and you're so with it, you get it. It's one thing if Minnie…and others, if they sign off later, but this is hard sledding here at the beginning. Like at ward level. Right? I'm sure you know. Anyway, thanks for all the help, but can we talk? I…" (OK, here was the moment...) "I really enjoyed our other sessions. I really like...," (nope, apparently not) "the way you see through some of the bullshit. And you're probably taking some risks yourself, with all this. God what a nightmare Mavis is!" (and here, just babbling, and he babbled on, relieved to be on a different pitch). "Anyway, I hope you're doing great, the other wards aren't too boring, hah, say Hi to Big Mary for me, and...call me, OK?"

Thus the situation was doubly acute. Doubly painful, as he creaked up the exterior wood stairs to his crap apartment after Day Four. Doubly blamable on Rhodes, perhaps. For actions and omissions both. The teetering, the canted stairs to the sorry brownness of his apartment, the fumbling with his key seemed the horrible correlatives of several indecisions.

Because she hadn't called back.

This was wounding in the obvious way, to the heart. And it had led to horrors of introspection, hollow hours of doubt which, this night, were to lengthen. In the maw of dark time, typical of this type of loss. Was it something about him? Something about her? But it was wounding in another way. Now, after three days, it seemed she wasn't even weighing in on his treatment plan project. Not even polite support. She was bailing! She was going political. She was going full-career heebie-jeebies. Someone had put the fear of God into her, Burns had set the snake on her, or else she'd gotten the jimjams about his project all by herself. In that career-saving way.

He was alone. And the only thing that allowed him four or five hours of sleep was that he didn't yet know the awful portent of Day Five.

Chapter 45

The next day, Thursday, soon provided an inkling. A little tinkling of the Horror Bell, just after the first smoking break. Burns had asked to see him.

Rhodes reflected that he had time to have some coffee, time to think. But this was interrupted by Van. "Fowler has a visitor."

"What!?"

"Not for him; she wants to see you, alone. Maybe she just wants to give him a nice message." Van's skepticism seemed to show that he knew Fowler didn't—or shouldn't—get visits.

"Is she there now?"

"Yeah. Make it quick."

The coffee was put down, the main door keyed, and Rhodes peeped around into the former TV bay of the adjoining, disused ward. This had been fixed up, with a throw rug and a few plants, for visitors.

"Mrs., Ms.?..."

"Hi. I'm Angeline. I'm Anson's sister."

"Well, great! I'm—"

"I know." She glanced around, kind of wrung her hands, which held something. "I'm a little nervous. I sort of talked my way in here. Anyway, I'm not seeing him."

She declined a chair. Rhodes blurted, "What's up with that? That he doesn't get visitors?"

"The family and I, you might have figured out…don't get along. That is, we don't agree about Anson. They put him here. A long time ago." She smiled in a self-deprecating way. "A long story!"

"Yeah, so I gather. Huh. Can you…enlighten me a little? About the past?"

"Oh…We gave tons of information at the time. About his manic episodes. It didn't amount to much, in a way. I mean in a troublesome way—in my view. But there was tons of detail…in what we gave them."

"There's nothing in his chart. His records—almost nothing."

She stood silently, looking quite a bit like her brother—tall, gray hair and eyes, the same fine nose and sharply cut upper lip. She seemed shy and, beyond that, hesitant about something. Was she going to say more?

"So here's why I came." And she held out a small envelope. Rhodes could feel right away that it was a key. "You can imagine, I…he's… taking some risk here. He said we could trust you."

"I give him this key?"

"Think what it implies. Think hard. This will have tremendous impact." She looked away. "Of course, you can say no. I'd rather know now. Be under no illusions—it's for a safe deposit box."

The other implications, beyond the contents of some bank box, were pretty obvious to Rhodes. They were echoed by still further rings of dire impact.

"The timing of this is important? He's expecting this?"

"Yes. And hoping, not expecting, that you'll help."

And the help, of course, went beyond just giving Anson the key.

Rhodes gulped. "OK. I'll give it to him." As she turned away, gracefully, but a little sadly, "Don't worry, I'll do it!"

The ward had been high for days. Davey Doucette, The Great Entertainer, still had to be checked every fifteen minutes, Long John more than once eluded his bathroom escort and had to be rounded up, a process that involved feet more than hands, and the Wild Man, still strapped down, was bellowing streams of florid nonsense.

Rhodes tried to collect his thoughts. He threw out the coffee that had gone cold, stood for a moment in the kitchen off the smoking area—just so he could be alone. He realized he needed to excuse himself with Van, to get to the Burns appointment. Things were starting, decidedly, to press in on him.

The ward itself had a tremulous feel. Its very air seemed to shudder. Its soul, if it had one left, trembled like a pot on a stove. As with the wall of his future, a shivering wall he'd felt himself flattened against, now Rhodes felt all the ward's psyche, like a quivering substance, thick around him. To be sure, a sensitive PHW would feel this, on a ward like the B, from time to time. But the present episode was amped up by grave personal issues. Impending ones.

"Van, I hafta go see Burns. 4:30, he told me to come."

"Is that right? With the ward in the state it's in? You didn't ask to see him—to, you know, get your way on a couple of things?" This was the least friendly version of Van Hoek that Rhodes had seen.

"Whoa, absolutely not. He needs to see me—probably, like, a probationary check." A dubious look from Van. "Well, to be honest, while I'm there I plan to hit him up. You know, for my thing, for the charting, we can't get anywhere without a little more from him on Fowler. So."

Van waved him off—plainly suspicious, about the Fowler sister among other things—and headed down the ward. Rhodes had five minutes to whip his thoughts into line and navigate the runnels of the massive Main Building.

"Hi!" he threw out, cheerfully, steering the spaceship straight into the black hole of the Burns universe. There was no answer. A clot of ivy over the window had further darkened the room, while a ray or two of sun made a silhouette of the M.D.'s massive head. In this black mass,

Rhodes, for the first time, was able to make out the eyes, like little cinders. They glowed and steamed like embers thrown into wet manure under a barn.

Right, slight exaggeration there. But there was a special tension in the room. The brown fish ventured to peek around Burns's left elbow.

"I'm not working this weekend," Burns began, in a neutral tone, "and you have a deadline." Taking a second to connect these two thoughts, Rhodes was trying to see how to venture into the dreaded topic when Burns added, "A deadline of Saturday. So perhaps you'll be good enough to slip a note under my door at the end of shift Friday. Tomorrow." Stated, not asked.

"Oh, right. So...*tomorrow*..."

"That going to be a problem?"

"OK, so, *interestingly*, I have a few—"

"I'll tell you what's interesting." This was flat out belligerent. "Aside from your *guh...* oo-wecent history." (Uh-oh.) "We'll get to that." Rhodes exhaled slowly and Burns warmed to his subject—though not, for some reason, with the ease of a polished orator or, for that matter, a boss. After a long pause, he launched into an unexpected explanation. "What is interesting, what could turn out to be a little *too interesting*, is that we have an External *guh...* oo-Weview coming up. And I may have mentioned that I have, we have, a bit of a credentialing problem in this Unit. In A Ward and B Ward. These are wards which will be the subjects of extra attention from the slimy—from the evaluators." Here the tone got a little plaintive, almost pleading. "We could look better. We, on paper and otherwise, we...look bad. Not just things that have happened—mostly before you came—but in the credentials area. I'd like..." here a long pause, some ceiling work, and a delivery that was suddenly a bit peristaltic, "I'd like to stay...in this position. Do the job...change the place."

Rhodes thought about what this meant, what Burns was trying to say. You couldn't fault him, it sounded reasonable. This wasn't to last.

"DAMN IT! I want to shape things up. Put Mavis on as full-time Supervising Nurse. I can get whatever I want out of Van Hoek, but I want you as charge on his days off. Then maybe you as day shift charge, as I've explained. You work well with Minnie, you can put a good face on things. We've been over this. You have a college degree for Christ's sake. I need...I need things to look better..."

"I understand. I get the picture. And thanks, I do appreciate it. But there's just one thing—"

"Oh *is that so*. What in the world could that be. After everything I've said, offered you. This *one thing*, that can be cleared up by tomorrow?"

"No, really, it can be, could be. Listen, I'm glad we're meeting because I would have come in anyway...on this thing. It's linked to a lot of issues on the ward, kind of...deficiencies, in the way we do things. For now, I just want to mention I'm working on a better system for notes in the charts. A way we can get much more—"

"Yeah fuck that."

"Excuse me?"

"I heard all about that. We have bigger fish to fry."

"We do?"

"You're not hearing me. Don't start *guh*... oo-weorganizing my ward on me. I need to LOCK IT DOWN! Get some of these patient behaviors, maybe some staff behaviors too, *tidied up*! OK? And I don't need anyone stirring Anson Fowler up either."

Rhodes hadn't mentioned Fowler. Where was this coming from? A dark foreboding stole into the room, as black as the massive head before him. Was Fowler, were all the patients, was Rhodes's treatment scheme going to disappear into the void of some other scheme of Burns's, some vast need from which no light or energy could ever escape?

"It's not stirring him up, it's—"

"You drop it! You hear me?"

What Rhodes *could* make out in the gloom was a finger, pointed at him like a fat little derringer in a poker game.

"I mean, it's not just about Fowler—"

"You know NOTHING about him!"

"Well, that's sort of my point. In fact, what I want to accomplish, with all the patients, what I'd be doing…er, in my position…if I stayed—"

"In *fact*, you'd be doing what I tell you. Damn it, how old are you? Don't you know how to act? Wait—is this about that nut house prep school? Has my f—, my sociopathic half-brother been twisting your arm? Well, has he?"

At this point two things had been introduced, too pointedly for what might have been—Oh Lord—a healthy and reciprocal discussion of the larger topic of Rhodes's staying. Something nagged at him about this trend. About where—as you might say—Burns was coming from.

"We don't have to go into that—"

"Yeah, and you don't have to go into that hellhole, never to emerge. Or to emerge a year from now, shit-canned, broken like a dry twig. Goddamn it, man! Can't you tell a lunatic when you see one?" The enormous man was suddenly on his feet, his chair yowling horribly as he shoved it back. All light was eclipsed. "Damn it, man! I stayed late for this meeting! Do you know he once set fire to a—"

"Alright," Rhodes gushed out, also rising. "Got my deadline, lots to think about. Hafta get back to the ward! Don't worry about a thing." Did he say that too placatingly? "Don't worry, I'll leave a note tomorrow! Don't worry!"

And he was off, at a dead run.

Back on the ward he wasn't able to connect right away with Anson Fowler. Fowler had his eye on him alright, but Rhodes had his eye on Billy Beans, who was crossing and recrossing in front of the kitchen door, artfully not looking at the instant coffee jar, retarded-sly. This was back before you said "developmentally-disabled-sly."

When Fowler sidled up to him later, it was a carefully chosen moment—they were alone. His eye contact was better than usual. There may even have been something playful in it. Hopeful, maybe, instead of angry. Rhodes tried for the tone of an old movie, "I believe I have something of yours." He didn't give him the key, but steered him a bit, something he was not usually able to do. "Let's walk down to the end of the ward."

When he handed it over, he said, without reflecting first, "I know what that is."

Fowler just looked at him. The beginnings of wild surmise.

"Let's say that this," as he handed it over, "is Act One. I don't suppose you care to share anything about Act Two?" This was met with silence. But Fowler's mental cogs were turning, and not in that spinning, stripping, wild way. Intelligence, planning. Weighing disclosures, risks.

What was Rhodes thinking? How far was Rhodes willing to commit himself? In fact, the reader should know that Rhodes's gears were turning almost in tandem.

Fowler committed himself. "I suppose Act Two would take some planning."

"Yes. Yes it would." They had reached the end of the ward. Had Rhodes, at this point, reached the end of a particular rope? Did *he* have some planning to do, of his own? The window at the end of the long corridor looked over much of the campus. All the red brick was lambent in the early evening sun. Peace and solace. The big old buildings gave Rhodes the same feeling he'd had looking down from the highway at Daniel Webster Academy in its little dell. To be part of such a thing. Or to be, forever, separate from it.

"Let's walk a bit more," he softly instructed his friend. "Slowly. Keep it casual."

Chapter 46

In his dream, Rhodes is flying over the hospital campus. He is piloting, through clouds of fluffy insouciance, his old Triumph car. Perhaps wingless, not that it matters—he's focused on the quaint dashboard gauges. The altimeter is of particular interest.

Thinking that he's perhaps too high, he guides the craft beneath a cloudbank, toward the shimmering roofs of the Main Building. One roof stretches long and wide before him, its slate tiles presenting a flat landing surface.

He competently flares his landing, bumps softly onto the roof, and taxis.

He finds he is barely able to brake adequately, just when he first sees the man at the far end, the man who makes slow arcane gestures with the fluorescent sticks, to guide the plane to a stop. As Rhodes rolls toward him, too fast, he can see the man is calm, the Day-Glow batons waving with great control.

Anson Fowler.

Chapter 47

Day Six. Though Rhodes knew some things were impending, he hadn't thought about the special zest of Fridays. This soon made itself felt.

There was no police presence—that would come later—but the light danced on the waxed floors like a gleeful bipolar. Van's face was tense, everyone else trying to get serious and match his intensity. During the four o'clock smokes, Mavis stood around and supervised, a bit unusual for a nurse. A knot began to form in Rhodes's stomach.

It was especially hard to get Anson Fowler in a quiet corner. The latter wore an anxious look all evening, though to the untutored it just looked like his long-simmering anger. One incident that bunged up his scheming was The Great Entertainer. The said showman trying to strangle himself with the tubes from the blood pressure cuff.

Galt was working this detail, usually routine. Somehow Doucette got the drop on him, and, in a suicide gesture well worthy of the name, whipped the rubber tubes around his neck. Sturdily built and raging, he had to be strapped down in the room just vacated by Roy Houle, who was now practically affable. So now frequent checks on him, along with the Wild Man, still trying to chew his thumb off, would be needed for the whole shift.

Rhodes was already pretty much in a clutching-his-skull mode, just before meds, when a giant was brought in by the capital city police. Woolly haired and bearded, bear-like under overalls. Though he was silent, his eyes were starting out of his sweaty head and his jaw was working in a strange way. Actual metal shackles, hand and foot. It was deemed best not to restrain him, but to lock him up. So he had to be stripped and checked for lice, and this on top of all the admissions paperwork and vital signs the Admissions Unit usually did.

"Y'all right there, partner?" Galt asked, with his wide grin, as they played a flashlight around the man's groin.

"Ecch...Oh, just Friday night jitters, I guess. We really could use an extra aide on weekends, you know."

"Yeah, and if we got one it would be Lenny. Right? So..."

"Right."

What had he worked out?

His thoughts were scrambling away from him, mice under the cabinets. As he stood by the medication door, helping Mavis, he processed the patients without looking at them, trying to bring back the previous evening.

Right. Fowler was going to have a medical emergency. Rhodes would take him to the Medical Building. He needed to speak to Fowler. The timing would have to be cute.

As Mavis locked the meds door, Jungle Jim started to go.

"C-c-c—"

"Hey! Cool it!"

"C-cu-cu-cu—!"

"Knock it off, Jim!"

"Cu-cu-cun—!"

"James!

Mavis wore no expression at all. A few feet away, he might as well have been clothes flapping on a clothesline. And he let out, at his highest pitch ever, with "CUNNINGLY PHRASED YET VOID OF MEANING!!"

Jaws dropped everywhere. Mavis stomped off as if nothing had happened. To everyone else, Jim's newfound grin and pop-eyes boded an uncharted journey. He folded his hands in his lap with an expression of supreme satisfaction. Mental gears spun everywhere. To Rhodes, the speech was perhaps a hermetic reference to inane hospital policy. Or to much of human endeavor. The PHWs girded up for a long evening.

The problem was...the *problem* that made Rhodes want to run down the ward, rip the screen off the end window, climb into the big elm outside and sit there chittering like a giant squirrel was that at that moment Colby the Shiteater was having a three course meal in one of the bathroom stalls. No time to shift blame and dive for cover—the three aides nearby, Rhodes among them, had to plunge after him. No amount of wipes, rubbing alcohol or hydrogen peroxide would ever make them clean again.

As they thrashed around in the bathroom, Long John was headed that way, with an escort of two. In a fiendish way, commensurate with the Friday night festivities, he skittered away from the door and sank his teeth into Moose's ankle. Moose, betraying no emotion, kicked him like a soccer ball—about fifteen feet. A door jamb stunned him enough that the herding and locking up went fairly smoothly, but then Moose had to be persuaded to lift his pant leg enough for them to see the wound. The skin hadn't been broken. One less bit of paperwork.

Van was getting tense, his head jerking from side to side in a way Rhodes hadn't seen before. He snarled at Rhodes when he saw the PHW reaching for Long John's chart, "None of this happened! The last ten minutes didn't happen, OK? I don't need it."

"Fair 'nuff," Rhodes agreed, anxious to go find Fowler.

But then, naturally, more problems. Someone noticed that Long John was lying in an odd way on the floor of his room. Van ordered vital signs. Breathing elevated, pulse a bit weak.

"Fuck!" was Van's medical opinion, at this point. "I'm calling Mavis. I don't want this on me."

They stood over Long John, with Mavis tapping her foot in deep thought. The moment when the average person would chew the lower lip, mulling things over. But her thin lips hardly ever moved.

Van said, "I'm worried about a hematoma. He hit that door pretty hard. How about I just send him up to City Hospital?"

Mavis thought some more. And Rhodes learned something valuable from what she said next. "They won't take him up there, from the ward. He'd have to go to the Medical Building—they'll take him from there."

"I don't want to do that. I can't spare an aide from the ward. Not the way things are."

"Just check his vitals every fifteen." And she clumped off the ward. Leaving, in her wake, a situation: now that she'd been called, and the injury discussed, Van would have to book the whole thing in the shift book, plus the Incident Report, plus the chart.

He went to the nurses' station slamming the bottom half of the Dutch-door, yelling over the top of it, "I'm cancelling breaks! No breaks tonight. I'll give you an extra ten minutes tomorrow, if you're on. Best I can do!"

On top of everything else Rhodes missed a Riot Bell for A Ward. He was changing the dressing on Wild Man's thumb ("My hands are limping around on the ceiling! Unbearable! Unhand me! As you can see, I'm strapped down here. Don't be obstreperous! Oh please!"), which he finished up in a flash, hearing Billy outside the door, going a bit high.

"Boo-WAH! Boo-WAH!"

Rhodes dodged Iggy, who had crafted an acrid kind of cackle meant to suggest he'd authored the whole wacky evening, and was intercepted running to the bell by Van.

"No! Just two going, I need people up here!"

This "I need people here" was troubling, a wrench in the gears.

Fowler was pacing like a psychotic emu in a zoo, and Rhodes wasn't sure how much the patient could take before he blew. He decided to give Van a few minutes to calm down, when the others came back from answering the bell. "Soon," he whispered to Fowler.

The standard greeting, "Ya lick the problem?" was tossed by Galt and met with mild amusement by Filbert and Knight, coming up from A Ward. They were sweating and in a great hurry to wash their hands. Rhodes didn't ask what horrors they'd encountered. He, too, was pacing now, trying to look busy, biding his time.

In mid-evening, he grabbed Fowler, put the patient's hand on his lower right belly, urged him to "Act like you're in pain. Go sit by the nurses' station."

"Hey Van, Fowler's been in a lot of pain. For hours. I'm getting worried."

"Jesus. You do vitals?"

Rhodes fibbed, "Yeah, pulse is kinda rapid." As Van hemmed and hawed, staring at the seated Fowler and wishing with every fiber of his psychiatric worker being that this problem would just go away, Rhodes added, "I'm thinking appendix. That's what I'm worried about."

"Naw. Come on!"

"Shit yeah. Man, we jump on it now, we're clean. It ruptures later in the shift, even on night shift, we have it all over our faces."

Van appeared to think this one over.

Rhodes had a great idea. "Hey! I have a great idea! I'm about to do Night Doors, I can shoot him over to the Medical Building while I do it. I can leave him there if that's what they want. At least they can check him out."

Van resisted, just because he was built that way, and also because he didn't want to lose a man.

"Plus, if there's anything wrong, they'll send him from Medical up to City Hospital. We can't send him from here—and his appendix blowing on this ward in the middle of the night...bad."

And, to be sure, Night Doors had to be done. You couldn't leave the place open all night. Any other aide would push back if asked to do them. "OK, do it. Try to get back soon. Leave him for diagnostics and run back, if you have to. I can call and get him later, or day shift can."

"You hear that, Anson? We're going on a road trip. I know you don't want to, but it's gotta be done. Come on, we'll walk slow, don't worry."

Just then he noticed Fowler had a new pair of slippers from the store room, and his pockets bulged strangely. Suddenly everything seemed childishly obvious, something they'd never get away with. When he glanced at Van, the charge aide was already scratching his head over the shift book.

Leaving the ward wasn't tricky—getting back would be. The walk to the tunnels was silent, damned odd to be anywhere but the ward with Fowler. Once in the tunnels, padding along on the packed earth, thoughts grew truly somber.

Fowler was hard to read. Tense, but with a boy's jumpiness. Or was Rhodes reading that positive note into him? What was Fowler thinking? When was his last sojourn away from the Stack? When was the last time he saw the leafy streets near the hospital? The last time he breathed air that didn't smell like floor wax? And his master plan—what of that?

Rhodes locked a few doors as they went. And his own thoughts? As we've seen, some of them swirled around Fowler, and a new vision of the man. A man in charge, a man headed somewhere. He pictured him ambling free in slippers with miles of good tread on them, sturdy hospital clothes—the plaid shirt, not the gray one—not too recognizable as such. In his pocket a shiny key to some great resource. At least one family member who cared about him. A mind fully capable of hiring someone to defeat any bogus committal orders. And a knot of anger loosening every day.

A set of possibilities, airy and open.

A future.

Ah, but Rhodes's other thoughts? They opened onto his own road. He makes it to the end of shift without being exposed, and he's a teacher. A purveyor of truths, sometimes sad ones, to upturned and largely sane faces. Once he has left his keys behind and is formally fired, the worst that can happen is a call from Burns to the half brother. This would be met with scorn by the headmaster—indeed, it would be considered a recommendation. Perhaps Rhodes and the H.M. would chuckle together over this bit. But no, the mental picture of such intercourse sends a shudder through the (still) PHW. He will just be sure to confirm his deal with Barnes, the very next day. And then have the rest of the summer off.

Pointing to a wire gate and the doors beyond it, he told Fowler, "I'll lock those later." He knew, and it sickened him in a way, that this was not the time to have a genuine and open conversation with the patient. They never had before.

"You can…wait here. I'll go down toward the Medical Building, like we said." He grinned at his own humor, tried, in the dark, to see his smile reflected. Fowler might have been smiling, just a little—in any case, he looked a bit lost. Rhodes walked a few steps, then turned back, "There's a pay phone in the store at the end of WicWas Street. Do you need any quarters?"

Fowler waved him off. And when Rhodes came back, when he turned that corner where tunnels met, Fowler was gone, as planned. And it was the end of something great, as he thought, something firmly believed, something courageous. Now a mite of his own courage was needed.

He would have to kill exactly half an hour, to make it plausible that Fowler had been checked out. That would bring it to nine o'clock—two hours of exposure on the ward. He also needed to update Van as quickly as possible, so that no call was made to the Medical Building. And take no chance with later calls. Dicey business. An earlier version of the plan, in which he confesses that Fowler has bolted from the tunnel and away, while Rhodes was trying to get the locks done, would have made for a much more unpleasant evening without (probably) being a fireable slip-up. He can always revert to this version, if it becomes a big deal after he has quit the place. The patient got away (as opposed to *was sprung*), and he was just too embarrassed to admit it. But this was the plan now, and Rhodes was alone with it, as alone as he'd ever been with anything.

The tunnel was empty and quiet. Rhodes soon found there was nothing to sit on—no ledge or utility box, no giant steam faucet, nothing. He paced the dank and grimy lengths of the tunnels he knew so well. If he'd been wearing slippers, and an aide from another building had seen him, he would have been yelled at, chased away.

Now up to the ward. Cautious peep around the smoking area door—the safer way in. Nobody. Quick check-in with Van. An effort to tell only one bald-faced lie all evening. "He's fine. They gave him an ultrasound, just indigestion. He's in his room early." (Right, two lies.) Rhodes looked busy, vigorously walking both wings of the ward, taking vital signs on the two who were in restraints. He shot the breeze for a while in the nurses' station. Then, full-blown panic. Van announced, a bit early, "OK, I'm doing census."

As casually as he could, Rhodes slipped out onto the ward. By pure luck Van didn't start on Fowler's wing. When the coast was clear, our heroic figure ducked into Fowler's room for the plan's last act. After a slight, desperate hesitation, he slipped into bed. He pulled the blanket over his head, but left one arm artfully dangling in plain sight. And waited.

An awful intimacy in this act, in this hour. Not in the degree of intimacy, but in the kind. A fear, perhaps like the fear Fowler had felt hundreds of times. Other patients, too. Rhodes hadn't been this afraid since he jumped off the garage roof on a dare at the age of eight. Or perhaps since that time he had suddenly thought Sherrill was simply bored by him—him and his plans. The fear that Van will pause, that the blanket will be pulled down, the flashlight played on his face. Peer-disgrace, Security called, a dénouement of searing embarrassments.

He looks at a rough patch on the wall, dimly present in the light from the hall. A horror resides there, as it resided all the days of Fowler's hospital life. Rhodes feels this more than he has ever felt it—more than in his almost weepy moments of sympathy for Doucette, Moose, and the others. A rich inversion, this. This is empathy, and he shudders with it.

The sleep pods are dim, the cavern dark. No idle chatter from the wardens, no pod to heat up in retribution. Up above in the pavilion there is silence. No pleasant bickering about epicurean notions. No aroma of sybaritic inventions. Out through the glass, the furrows stretch empty of life. No one is being browbeaten, goaded or punished. The humus lies unturned, the fields lie fallow, and red. The struggle for control has abated with one last setting sun.

Van pauses. The light plays around the room. Fowler, perhaps, feels the asphalt sidewalk under his slipper as he steps off a lawn.

Van moves on.

A short time later—patients are in bed, staff busy writing in the charts—Rhodes bundles bedclothes, some laundry and a paper bag or two into something like a body under the blanket, and shows up to do his share of the charts. With great relief he sees that Fowler's isn't among those left to do. He buries his nose in his work.

At 10:30 he's starting to unwind. Night shift is notoriously casual about bed checks. Twenty minutes to go. Van is dripping sweat onto the shift book. Dying for this hell-shift to end. The others are making their useless doodles in the charts. Rhodes surveys their placid faces, from which all feeling has been syphoned. To be fair, in just a few minutes, they will be real, perhaps kind, to those around them—they're meeting in a bar at the edge of town. When they go home, they may swell with humanity, kisses, pats on the head. Good listening skills. But now, no. The hospital did this to them, though they own some part of it. Their incuriosity, inability to feel anything for eight hours, unwillingness to change.

Just keep the head down, get going on Doucette's chart.

There's the self-strangulation to chart. And what *about* these notes, this incident? Well, why not? The reader may judge—is it a final Fuck You! to everyone, or simply of a piece with his abiding sincerity, that he charts it his way?

O.: *Patient attempted to strangle himself with tubes from blood pressure apparatus. Appeared extremely sad, as of late, and the action <u>seemed</u> more than a gesture (though no chance of completion). (How do the untrained know when it's a gesture. What do the initiated mean by the arrogant bit of jargon, "gesture.")*

A.: *Patient continues in a very low phase. This action shows more energy and purpose than has recently been observed. It's possible that this is the beginning of a swing toward high energy, hyper manic phase. If so, some danger of increased energy for a suicidal act. Somebody please read this. Actually read this.*

P.: *Perhaps reexamine chart, or <u>obtain more history from psychiatric staff</u>, to see what suicide attempts have been made in the past. Engage patient in discussion of this incident. Try to chart where he is in his manic-depressive cycle. All shifts coordinate on this, good God. Perhaps check blood lithium.*

Can't everyone—PHW to Unit Director—meet once on this? Like a team? No?

H. Rhodes PHW 1

And soon it is 10:50. An escape, and the last goodnight of a flamed-out career. Quick note to Burns, calm and politic. Because he has promised. Then down to The Alibi. To drink—as few mental health workers (and they are stalwart imbibers) have ever drunk before.

The Heart's Epilogue

And so…what can you do?

You stagger on, always in the middle of a vast convocation of idiots, always parting them, trying for an opening in the throng—so you can see the right path. But every divergence of paths is equally fraught. It's as if you learn nothing.

Certainly, "upon mature reflection," as the saying goes, you have learned that one shouldn't append a rant about the state of humanity to a well-considered narrative such as this. At least, one should have gained some damned maturity. But to do this, you'd have to have made headway, right, in fresh tides of lazy charlatans, violent surges of serve-serving drones, towering new waves of control-fetishists and power-mad martinets. Right?

What to do? Just when the radical firebrand head says, "Yes! Go for it! Pull it all down!" the heart weighs in.

But is its counsel wise?

"Carry on, lad. Be not pulled from the path. All is love!"

Rhodes jets up the highway to the prep school, to a new vision, with tall poplars on either side, in their timorous applause.

PETER THOMPSON'S publications comprise 25 books of poetry, fiction (and translations of both), songbooks, two anthologies of French literature, along with critical projects. His major translating effort has been six works by the great Algerian author Nabile Farès, including his *Discovery of The New World.*

Thompson is a literature and language professor at Roger Williams University and edits *Ezra: An Online Journal of Translation.*

He also worked for many years in mental hospitals in three states. The story of his character, Harrison Rhodes, continues in the novels *Winter Light* and *Harrison's Word.* Information on books at www.peterthompsonbooks.com.

Praise for *Harrison's Word* —

Peter Thompson's work is always assured and can take a reader from the profane to the sublime. It's provocative and poetic, and funny and sometimes discomfiting. In his man Harrison Rhodes, Thompson explores ego, uncertainty and hope in someone who, like the rest of us, struggles with all of those.

—Ted Delaney, author of *Broken Irish*

Praise for *Winter Light* —

An acton-packed romp as the Latin teacher Rhodes maneuvers the absurd banalities and long winter of a New England prep school. Thompson's writing is fresh and irreverent, keenly intelligent with flashes of light and music.

—Sonja Livingston, author of *Ghostbread*

Practical vs. Reckless. Confused vs. Focused. Conformist vs. Renegade. In *Winter Light*, Peter Thompson's protagonist, Rhodes, embodies these various opposing and conflicted psyches that have defined the idea of yearning within the modern American novel. And through them, Rhodes certainly takes his place among that cast of unsettled, well-meaning yet troubled characters of the literary landscape—standing alone in the fields, parting the weeds, and trying to spot their dream.

—Adam Braver, author of *November 22, 1963*

Running Wild Press publishes stories that cross genres with great stories and writing. RIZE publishes great genre stories written by people of color and by authors who identify with other marginalized groups. Our team consists of:

Lisa Diane Kastner, Founder and Executive Editor
Mona Bethke, Acquisitions Editor, Editor, RIZE
Benjamin White, Acquisitions Editor, Editor, Running Wild Press
Peter A. Wright, Acquisitions Editor, Editor, Running Wild Press
Rebecca Dimyan, Editor
Andrew DiPrinzio, Editor
Cecilia Kennedy, Editor
Barbara Lockwood, Editor
Cody Sisco, Editor
Chih Wang, Editor
Pulp Art Studios, Cover Design
Standout Books, Interior Design
Polgarus Studio, Interior Design
Nicole Tiskus, Production Manager
Alex Riklin, Production Manager
Alexis August, Production Manager

Learn more about us and our stories at www.runningwildpress.com

Loved these stories and want more? Follow us at
www.runningwildpress.com, www.facebook.com/runningwildpress,
on Twitter @lisadkastner @RunWildBooks @RwpRIZE